The Storytellers' Club

The Storytellers' Club

THE PICTURE-WRITING WOMEN OF THE ARCTIC

Loretta Outwater Cox

ALASKA NORTHWEST BOOKS®

Anchorage, Alaska ▪ Portland, Oregon

Library of Congress Cataloging-in-Publication Data

Cox, Loretta Outwater.
 The storytellers' club : the picture-writing women of the Arctic /
Loretta Outwater Cox.— 1st ed.
     p. cm.
 Includes bibliographical references.
 ISBN 0-88240-607-8 (hardbound)
 1. Inupiat women—Fiction. 2. Women storytellers—Fiction. 3. Storytelling—Fiction.
4. Alaska—Fiction. I. Title.

 PS3603.O923S76 2005
 813'.6—dc22
2005009980

First edition 2005

Alaska Northwest Books®
An imprint of Graphic Arts Center Publishing Company
P.O. Box 10306, Portland, Oregon 97296-0306
503-226-2402; www.gacpc.com

President: Charles M. Hopkins
General Manager: Douglas A. Pfeiffer
Associate Publisher: Sara Juday
Editorial Staff: Timothy W. Frew, Tricia Brown, Jean Andrews,
            Kathy Howard, Jean Bond-Slaughter
Production Staff: Richard L. Owsiany, Susan Dupere

Editor: Ellen Wheat
Designer: Andrea Boven Nelson, Boven Design Studio, Inc.
Cover illustration: Bob Crofut
Map illustration: Debra Dubac (Dubac Designs)

Printed in the United States of America

For Anthony L. Cox,

Yolanda Marie Cox White,

Katherine M. Cox,

and

Christopher O. Cox—

our children

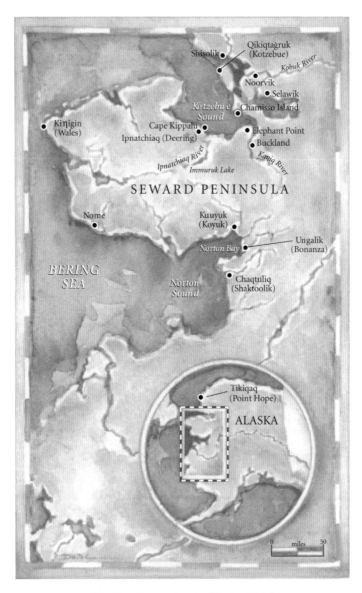

The Northwest Arctic *[Early 1900s]*

Contents

ACKNOWLEDGMENTS

In the summer of 1983, my parents shared their memories and stories with me while we were living in Nome, Alaska. Perhaps what came across strongest among the stories was my father, Walter's, appreciation for his grandmother Sikkitkoq, who took care of him when he was a little boy.

I also want to thank my mother, Ruth, for the traditional oral stories she told her children, such as "The Chief's Daughter," "Pisiqsuqliq," "The Story of the Three Giants," and "The Beluga Hunt," which I have included in this book.

I wish to acknowledge the following people who have passed away: Martha Hunnicutt, Friends Church missionary, who documented the early life of Qutleruq, one of my great-grandmothers; Lily Savok, my grandmother, whose picture-writings were the basis of the Storytellers' picture-writings. I have always had such great admiration for the Storytellers and their lives—thank you. It was recently said that the Malemiut Inupiaq had the greatest degree of respect for one another, and I hope that this is clearly conveyed throughout this book.

My thanks go to Solomon Elook, who told the Inuquin story to my brother.

My appreciation goes to Ellen Wheat, whose editorial work has been invaluable for this book.

A NOTE TO THE READER

The year I was born, in 1944, my parents sent my older sister Theresa to live with our grandparents, John and Lily Savok, in Ipnatchiaq. Theresa clearly remembers Lily and her friends using picture-writing to teach stories from the Bible.

In 1899, Lily's parents, Qutleruq and Egaq, had taken Lily down to Unalakleet to attend the Swedish Covenant Church run by missionaries. While Lily attended school there and studied the Bible, she drew what were called mnemonic picture signs, or "picture-writing," so she could convey the lessons to her parents, who could not read or write. The Storytellers in this book, women from Ipnatchiaq, learned picture-writing from Lily, and used it to communicate and to pass down their stories and ways, as an extension of traditional Native oral history.

One of the Storytellers, whose name was Emma Sikkitkoq Mills, or Sikki, was my father's grandmother.

1

It was the beginning of the dark season, those months of November through February when the sun leaves the sky. Sikki was happy that some of her friends were coming over for Storytelling. She had already prepared a brew made from Labrador tea she had picked on the tundra in the summer. There was a fragrant aroma in her house, and the kerosene lamp made soft shadows on the sod walls. Every time she and her friends got together, it was a time to visit, laugh, and tell each other stories. This time it would be her turn to be the Storyteller, and her friends would listen. They had agreed that whoever was hosting the group would be the Storyteller. Sometimes, the schedule changed if a Storyteller told stories they wanted to hear again and again. This season Sikki had been telling great stories, they all agreed.

Today, the Storytellers in attendance were Utoyuq, whose familiar name was Uto, Panehuq (or Panea), Nupanraq (or Nupa), Ayichak (or Ayi), and Neġroġruq (or Ne). As the women came through the little wooden door, Sikki, whose formal name was Sikkitkoq, welcomed each one and made her feel important. Sikki had a way of doing that, always with contagious laughter. Each woman was handed a cup of tea as she came in, and from all the times before, each had her own special place to sit on the floor of the cozy sod home.

By this season, Sikki had collected six tin cups. Since she had returned to the village, she had trapped six red fox and was able to trade each pelt for a tin cup at the local trading post. As for where she had been, she planned to tell that story one day. But for now, she was proud of her six tin cups.

Sikki and Panea had started the Storytellers' Club. It happened naturally, as they always visited each other after their nets were set side by side in the river behind the village. Panea lived by the mouth of the river, and Sikki lived just a few yards farther in. Of all the Storytellers, they saw each other more often because of their places to set their nets. Fishing customs had been started by their ancestors, and now the places to set the nets belonged to them. When the two women were out at the same time, and if no other family member was there to help, they helped each other. As they waited for fish to get caught in the net, they would build a fire. Living by the ocean, there was never a shortage of driftwood for the fire. During their days at the seashore, they planned to start the Storytellers' Club for when the days got dark and cold, when they would invite their friends over.

After the first meeting of the Storytellers' Club, the women agreed that they would trade furs for the pencils sold at the trading post. They would trade one of the sealskins that they knew they would be getting in the fall. Working together, the women had collected eight indelible lead pencils. The pencils were a mixture of gypsum, black lead, and silver nitrate. Gypsum made the compound hard and impervious to atmospheric moisture, lead was the coloring agent, and silver nitrate caused the lead to turn black when exposed to heat or light. Licking the lead caused it to soften and spread when applied.

Every fall, each person who had a seal net would hunt or fish at his or her own special place. The right to hunt or fish at that spot on Kotzebue Sound was handed down through the generations beginning long before 1816, when the place was named by a German explorer. There was a bluff, called Kippalu, located about three miles to the west of the village of Ipnatchiaq, and near that bluff they set their seal nets.

The nets were set straight out, one after another, about six or seven in all. There were no arguments among the people, since each family knew where its place was. One family's net would be set starting from the shore. Then the next person's net would be set with a rock anchor straight out from the first net, and so on. The men would use a *kayaq* as the nets were set farther out from the shore.

Important to Sikki was the memory of preparing the seal hides to make these nets. The nets were made from the hides of bearded seals, or *ugruk*, that were caught in the spring. After all the seal meat was hung to dry and the blubber was set to render, the skins were prepared for making rawhide to weave into nets. It was a two-person job, and Sikki and her husband, Utli, or Utliniq, always worked together. While she held the prepared skin away from him, Utli skillfully pulled the skin into strips, measuring with his thumb. Utli was gone now, but Sikki had her memories.

The atmosphere in Sikki's home was filled with respect because that was first of all what the people felt about each other. It was a way of life. That was the rule and the law that they lived by, necessary for their people to survive. Sikki thought of this again as each member of the Storytellers came to her house. A woman would knock on Sikki's little wooden door. The visitor would not touch the handle to open the door until Sikki said, "Come in." Then, when the visitor entered, she stood by the door until Sikki told her to come in and sit down.

After Sikki checked to see that everyone was there, she passed the pencils around. The indelible pencils were kept in an old clay pot that belonged to her mother, Ekiyuq. Then she started tearing pieces of the packaging paper they had collected from Magid's store. When someone went to trade for something, the storekeeper wrapped the item in brown paper that came off a huge roll and tied the parcel with white cotton string. With all of them collecting paper, they had enough for their picture-writing.

I'm glad the Native church people started teaching us the Bible by using picture-writing, Sikki thought. Now, my friends and I can have fun telling our stories to one another.

Sikki then addressed the Storytellers, saying she had a lot to tell them today. Before she began drawing, she made sure all the Storytellers' cups of tea were full. To begin, she made eight dots on her piece of paper. Then each of them made eight dots. She could see everyone begin by wetting the pencils with their tongues, so that the pencils would write. That's why they needed their cups of tea, because the pencils needed to be licked by a wet tongue.

Sikki started her story.

"In the year 1887, I was eight years old," she said. "The village of Deering then just had an Inupiaq name, Ipnatchiaq. There were only a few families living here then." Sikki drew a straight line. And then all the Storytellers drew a line, each one wetting her pencil with her own saliva.

"This line represents the seashore," Sikki told them. She remembered a sandy beach with smooth rocks. The ocean, since time immemorial, had cuddled each rock, smoothing out the jagged edges. The rocks were so smooth you could walk comfortably on the beach without your *mukluks.* So when a person walked barefoot, she got a foot massage, and depending on the temperature of the day, she got either a warm one or a cool one. This was during the summer," she said to them.

"You could only see rocks and sand on the shore. There were no clams or any sign of seaweed until low tide," Sikki said. "But once the tide got very low, my cousin Qutla and some other children of the village would run and play on the sandbars. We would run after little creatures called *putuguqseeyuqs,* or 'toe lovers.' The others knew that these creatures looked like scorpions, only smaller, and had a light mint green color.

"Sometimes, a small piece of seaweed could be found, but we never did anything with it, just noticed it," Sikki continued. "Sometimes, we found a clump of black elongated shells. Those mussels were not a staple diet for those who lived here because there weren't enough of them. But when the kids found some, they would eat them raw; they were chewy and salty.

Sikki's Picture-Writing: *Ipnatchiaq and Wild Celery*
[DRAWING BY LORETTA OUTWATER COX]

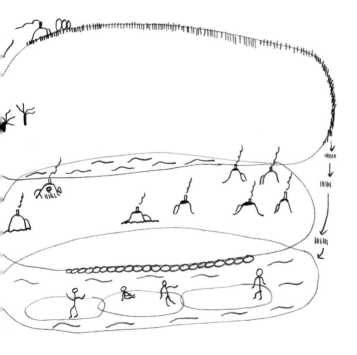

"Most of the time, when the tide was low, there was an east wind. That wind was warm and it blew the waves so that a white foam formed and got blown about on the sandbars."

At this point, Sikki stopped and drew three ovals that overlapped. The three ovals meant the ocean, the earth, and the sky. But they also signified the three sandbars. It was Sikki's philosophy at this stage of her life that things happened in threes.

"There was a sandbar that day due to the sky pulling on the ocean and showing more earth," she said. "It was just a borrowed moment from the sea." Sikki remembered how she and her friends were thankful that the ocean had brought them that good summer day.

"When there was an east wind like that, the water of the ocean was green," Sikki told the Storytellers. "I have always wondered what was green in the east. When I was little, I imagined that far, far away, wherever the east wind came from, everything was green."

She stopped and drew a dome like her house. Then she drew three circles meaning a father, a mother, and a child. Below the house, she put marks all the way across, and drew two more rows, one in the middle and one across the sky.

"The marks mean green grass," Sikki explained. "Wherever the east wind came from, everything was green. When it arrived at Ipnatchiaq, it turned the ocean green. Otherwise, every day the ocean was blue. If the sky was blue, then that was the color of the water. If the sky was gray, then the ocean was gray. On those days, especially when the ocean was blue, you could smell the ocean. It had its own smell, like salt, only it took you into it. When you were there, you felt a sense of peace, that everything was okay in your world, and you didn't want to be anyplace else. The ocean said to you, 'You belong to me. I will feed you and your people. If you live by me and keep me company, I will carry driftwood to you from the rivers so that you can have warmth. With this driftwood, you also can build your shelters.'

"The ocean could also be humble because it said, 'The only thing I can't bring is water to drink. But I can work with the wind to create rain clouds to bring you water.'

"It is so wonderful to live by the ocean," Sikki said.

The village of Ipnatchiaq, now called Deering, is located on a strip of land that has the ocean to the north and a small river flowing parallel to the coast behind it. When you follow the river upstream, it becomes a narrow creek. Another river flows from the south and connects with the small river at the tip of the strip of land. Although the salty ocean is only a few yards from the little river, the water in the river is not salty, so the people could use it for household needs. The villagers went farther up the river that flowed from the south to get water for drinking.

Sikki wet her pencil and drew the strip of land with the two rivers joining together east of the village. Then on the strip of land, she drew eight small ovals signifying the peoples' sod houses. Her family's sod house and Panea's sod house were on the back side of the strip of land, whereas the other houses were on the ocean side with lots of space between them.

Sikki continued her story. "Across the big river was a perfect hill. In the wintertime, my cousin Qutla and I would take part of a sealskin to use to slide down the hill. Sometimes Qutla's family visited in the wintertime. The hill was big enough to make you really tired by the time you walked to the top, and it gave you a long ride down to the bottom. But something was strange about that hill in the summer. No berries grew there and the people didn't use that hill for any purpose. In contrast, the tundra and the rolling hills on the western side of the village were used for picking greens and berries, and the bluff at the far end, called Kippalu, was full of life in the summertime, with thousands of seagulls, eider ducks, and puffins."

Sikki told the Storytellers that what she liked most about this place they called home was that there were no trees. "There were only willows and they were located up the big river." As she talked, she drew willows at about a quarter mile up the river. She also drew willows along the way to the bluff called Kippalu. On those willows (*Salix* species), she drew leaves to signify the leaves that they picked in the springtime.

"We can't forget how important those leaves are for our health," she reminded the others. "Those leaves give us sunshine when it is no longer here. Because we eat so many of the leaves, our skin is smooth, our hair is strong, and our fingernails stay strong to help us with our work."

Sikki smiled at her friends and said, "There's not one homely person sitting here." And because the people love to laugh, they looked at one another and began to giggle.

"When I was eight, our houses were almost the same as they are now. The three main differences now are the doorways, the windows, and the stove," she continued. "When I was small, our house entrances were different. We had to crawl down a little tunnel to get in, and in the winter a big sealskin hung there as a door to keep out the cold. Now we have a wooden door with a latch to keep it shut. And it is at ground level.

"Our light came from the top of the sod house. The window was made from beluga intestines sewed together to let the light through. It was rainproof and lasted a long time. But you couldn't see out the window. Now we have this amazing glass window, and I can watch the river and look out to see what the weather is doing.

"And now we have these little woodstoves to keep us warm. At that time, we did not have the oil drums that the gold miners bring nowadays. Our menfolk learned to cut up the oil drums to make woodstoves.

"When I was small, our light and our warmth came from the oil lamp," and she pointed to it. "I keep mine. It was the one my mother, Ekiyuq, had. In those days, we didn't really need an airhole, but we had one to look outside. Our oil lamp didn't smoke, and I always wondered how our ancestors invented that. Now we have a kerosene lamp, and sometimes when I forget to turn the wick down, it smokes and stinks up my whole house." And with those words, she checked her kerosene lamp.

Sikki told the Storytellers it was time for a break, and that they would go out and check the weather. When Sikki came back in, she made more tea. Her hot water was ready on the stove, so it didn't take long for the tea to steep, and she refilled all their cups.

Ready to draw again, the Storytellers picked up their pencils and proceeded to wet them from their mouths.

"Draw the hill that is across the river on the east side," Sikki said. "Then continue drawing the hill with a bluff against the ocean. Then keep drawing the hill with a long slope until you reach another river.

"Make that river flow from the south," she continued. "Across the river is another hill, and in front of it, by the ocean, is the spot where my family and Qutla's family spent time together in the fall when berry picking was over. My mother, Ekiyuq, and Qutla's mother, Paneluq, were second cousins. Qutla's family lived in another village a day's travel to the east. Their village was a long way up the river in a place with lots of spruce trees."

"When our families arrived at this spot by the ocean, we all cleaned out the shelter," Sikki told them. "Our two families met there just about every summer, and the shelters we used were there long before Qutla and I were born. They were halfway down in the ground, just like the ones we had in our village. Every fall when we met there, we'd have to do some repair work because maybe a piece of wood had caved in or little animals had lived in the place for a while.

"I was so happy to see my cousin Qutla again. First we would explore the beach to see whether anything interesting had washed up on shore. Many different shapes of wood had drifted in over the year, and by the end of the day, the two of us would have gathered lots of pieces that our parents could use to carve different household utensils or floats for nets. In those days, most of our bowls were made from wood we collected.

"Another day, Qutla and I would inspect every rock on the beach looking for ones with holes in them. Rocks with holes were useful as net sinkers.

"In those days, no one was in a hurry," Sikki recalled. "Children did not go to school. They learned to become good, contributing members of society by observing what their parents did.

"There was lots of activity and storytelling in the men's *qasgi*, which was a meeting house for men and for the young boys learning to make all the gear for the hunt. Boys watched and listened to the men, but mostly to the one that each would emulate. It was of utmost importance for the men to behave in an upright and just way, since they never knew when they were being watched by the boys.

"The girls observed the women in their lives, to learn," she said. "They knew that the women were the 'stitch makers,' meaning that they would carry the burden of keeping everyone in their family clothed for all seasons. But of greater significance, the women were taught to intuitively keep everything together. Men were the 'keepers of the tradition,' and therefore they were thought to be the most important. The women let them think this, but the women knew that if it weren't for them, doing all the hard work putting up supplies to feed the family and planning for the future, the people wouldn't survive." Sikki pointed out to the Storytellers that she had not always known this. But now that she was in her fifties, she had reached this conclusion as she reflected on her life.

Continuing, Sikki said, "There was no waiting around once we got there. We knew we had to get started, gathering the clay to use for making pots. My mother's cousin Paneluq was an expert at making pots. It took lots of time to make the pots and to bake them, enough pots for all members of the community. We always found the clay in the same spot, and every year there was the same amount of clay—it was never diminished no matter how much clay we used. The clay was the color of the skin of a bearded seal, or *ugruk*, once the hair was taken off, a dark gray color.

"All the adults, both men and women, would dig the clay from the ground," Sikki remembered. "We didn't have shovels then, so we dug the clay with a small, sturdy rock, which worked better than a large, thin rock because it was faster. After a considerable amount of clay was dug, it was put on a big *ugruk* skin. The adults would work together to mix the clay.

"At this point in the process, Qutla's mother, Paneluq, would knead in ptarmigan down that she had collected that year. There were many ptarmigan where she lived, and all winter long she collected down from the ptarmigan her husband brought home. He set snares where the ptarmigan made tracks in the snow. She stored the down in a beluga stomach she had made into a container. Everyone mixing the clay would grab a handful of down to fold into the clay. Down was added to strengthen the clay that would be made into pots, cups, bowls, small dishes, and lamps. After working all afternoon mixing and then taking a lunch break, the creative process would begin.

Sikki told the Storytellers that back then, they shaped the pots with their hands. "They made large serving platters to use on the table for a big meal. They made pots that were used to heat water; they were smaller so that it wouldn't take long for the water to heat up. My mother used her lamp's flame to slowly warm the water," Sikki told them.

"Both my mother and Paneluq knew what needed to be done and told everyone what they should make," Sikki explained. "That year, when I was eight, Qutla and I were told to roll out lots of little clay beads. We made as many as a hundred of them. When we finished rolling the beads, Paneluq showed us how to make a hole in each one, so that a piece of skinny rawhide could go through. Every little girl in the two villages would have beads for her hair in the coming year. The work made us feel special. I will never forget when I was eight," Sikki said, with a smile.

As the Storytellers made pictures on their pieces of brown paper, Sikki told them, "My mother and Paneluq drew stick figures on the pots they made to record who was there at the time. Ekiyuq would draw herself, her husband, and me. Paneluq would draw her husband, and my cousin Qutla, and herself. They also drew the extended family members who were present, especially ones who were useful and not lazy.

"When all the pots were molded," she continued, "they started firing them right away. The pots were piled up under a mound of driftwood, which they set on fire. It was a big bonfire, and they kept it burning all night and all the next day, until the pots had baked to a useful hardness. It was good to have those young extended family members, to help tend the fire. Especially the young people, who are the same everywhere—they love to stay up late." Sikki wet her pencil to draw a big fire, and all the Storytellers did the same.

Sikki returned to her story. "In that area, a little way up the river and to the east, a lot of wild celery grew. Each year, the people waited until the plants had almost died back before they harvested them for medicine. We dug up the roots and stored them as medicine to treat a bad cold. You could chew on the raw root or you could boil it and then drink the broth. Or you could cut the stem into bite-size pieces and chew on it to relieve a sore throat. The older this plant was, the stronger it was. This same plant was also picked early on for eating. It was stored away for the winter, and mixed with willow leaves in seal oil." Sikki drew the tall wild celery plant.

Sikki then told the Storytellers that she would finish the day with a story that had been passed down to her from her mother's cousin Paneluq.

Once upon a time, a chief's daughter was engaged to a good hunter. One day, this hunter went hunting out on the ocean. He paddled out in his *kayaq* and he didn't come back. The chief's daughter cried and cried. She took no comfort from the people who tried to console her.

One day, a little orphan girl went to her and kept her company just by being there. Eventually, the orphan girl encouraged her to eat. Being a chief's daughter, she had everything to eat including delicious caribou marrow. She was so pampered that she even had enough marrow to oil her hair and give it a shine. The orphan girl went quietly about her business. She shined the chief's daughter's hair with some bone marrow, because she thought it might cheer her up.

Springtime came. The orphan girl found out that some young women were going on a picnic. They were going somewhere in an *umiaq.* So the orphan girl arranged for the chief's daughter and her to go along. The orphan girl knew they would honor her request in an attempt to make the chief's daughter happy.

When they reached their destination, all the other girls were laughing and were happy to be outdoors. The orphan girl did not leave the chief's daughter's side. As they were taking a short walk, they found huge wild celery stalks. When they pulled one out of the ground, it came out without any difficulty. The roots and all just came right up, leaving a big hole in the ground.

The two girls were amazed at the size of the hole. When they looked down, they saw another country below the ground. The chief's daughter immediately saw the man she had been engaged to when he disappeared. She thought about what a good hunter he had been and how he knew all about the ocean. Now she knew that he had fooled everyone. The ocean did not take him; he had used the ocean to deceive everyone.

The chief's daughter was determined to find out why he had done that. So she turned herself and the orphan girl into spiders. They communicated in spider ways, and both tied the end of their spiderweb to the celery root hole, and traveled to the country down below, to spy on the people who lived there.

While they were observing the ocean in that country, they noticed a *kayaq* on the water. They both recognized the hunter. After landing his *kayaq* on shore, he pulled a seal onto the beach.

The two spiders watched a girl meeting the hunter. She carried a wooden ladle full of water, because it was the custom to pour water down the throat of a dead seal so it could have one last drink to make it to the spirit world of the seal. After that, you could start cutting up the seal.

That night, the two spiders crawled to positions in the hut so they could spy on the couple. It came as a surprise to the chief's daughter that this good hunter had been taken by force just because this girl needed someone to hunt for her. She waited until it was nighttime to reveal herself to him. Seeing her came as a shock to him and he wondered whether it was a dream.

The second night, the chief's daughter again assumed human form and motioned for the man to come to her. She quietly told him the story of how she and the orphan girl came to this country under the ground. And that there were two spiderwebs tied to the other world to help them get back. She told him that all three of them would leave that very night, and she told him where to meet the two spiders. He still loved the chief's daughter, and he desperately wanted to go back with her.

When he got to the place where they would go up to the other world, she magically turned him into a spider. They quietly climbed up the spiderwebs and reached their world. So with the help of the orphan girl, the chief's daughter brought the hunter back, and they lived happily ever after.

It was said that when you do the right thing, you can put your world back together again like the chief's daughter did.

With that, Sikki said, "*Tavra*."

~~~~~~~

One of the Storytellers asked Sikki if she would like to have the next session at her house again.

Sikki was thankful to be asked, and said, "Yes, I would, and maybe a few more times after that." But it was the custom of the people not to sound greedy, so she asked whether anyone else wanted to have the session at her house. She knew that each of the Storytellers had lots of good stories to tell.

All the five women had on simple parkas that were made of squirrel. Because it was winter, they wore the parkas with the hair side in, to keep warm. As they walked to the little wooden door, each one said "thank you" in their Malemiut dialect, "*Quyana.*"

2

Utli and Walter

When Sikki worked on her fishnet, she would think often of Utli, who had been her husband. It was easy to reminisce when she was weaving the loops of the net. Early in the morning after she had her morning tea, she would often start her fishnet work by unraveling a flour bag. She sat down at her favorite spot in her house, in front of the one window she had. The window faced up the river. Since it was winter now and the river was frozen, she could see an occasional dog team go by, probably heading out to hunt for ptarmigan or to go up the river for clean ice for drinking and cooking.

To begin her work on a flour bag, she could easily find the beginning of the thread in the fabric because she had worked on so many bags. Taking the start of the thread, she would unravel the bag, winding the thread around a carved wood spindle so she could use the string easily when weaving her fishnet. She had searched the beach for a piece of driftwood that was just the right size for a spindle to carve and to hold her flour bag string.

On the white flour bags, the large word FLOUR was stamped in red. Sikki didn't know what the letters meant because she had not attended school. It was only when her grandson Walter started going to school that he told her what some of the letters were. On the same bag there were other smaller words and they were stamped in blue. As she unraveled the bags, she could watch the letters and words disappear. And her string would be red, white, and blue.

At Walter's schoolhouse, she could see a red, white, and blue banner hanging on a pole. The flour bags reminded her of the banner. Walter told her that in school, they called it a "flag," and that the teacher made the kids stand up and say something to it every morning when they started class.

When all the string of a bag was unraveled and wound onto the spindle, she began to make twist braids out of it by first cutting three long pieces. Sikki made twist braids by rubbing one piece of string on her cheek and then holding it as she twisted the other two. Then she would let two of the strings unwind onto the other, and let the last string unwind around the first two. The braided strings from the flour bag became a sturdy twine for weaving a fishnet. As she looked at her net this morning, it was about five feet long, and it was white, red, and blue.

No one else in the village was making a fishnet out of flour bags. So when they found out that Sikki was making a net like that, they donated their empty flour bags to her. She was grateful, and when she thought about all the fish she would be getting with her new net, she knew she would share her catch because that was the custom. And it was a custom she was teaching her grandson Walter—to share everything.

In winter, Walter watched her share all the tomcod that she caught through a hole in the ice. Sikki loved to go ice fishing all day when tomcod were in abundance. Walter would be at school in the middle of town, and she knew what time to be home so she could be there when he got home. Tomcod are about eight to ten inches in length, Sikki reflected. You can hook them easily with a little hook that has beads attached to it. When it's cold, the fish stay fresh when stored in a gunnysack.

Sikki prepared tomcod in a variety of ways. One day, she would boil them and drink the broth. The next day, she would fry them in her cast-iron frying pan that she traded for at the fair across the bay. But the most delicious way to eat them was to dip frozen chunks into seal oil. And if she got a lot in the spring-time, like in April, she would string up the fish with beach grass to dry. Throughout the village, you could see garlands of tomcod hanging on the caches.

She looked forward to having a lunch of dried tomcod when she went berry picking in the summer. Before she could eat some of the dried fish, she would have to pound it, because the drying process made the fish hard as rock. Dried tomcod tastes like crab and makes a delicious meal, Sikki thought.

When Sikki worked on her fishnet made out of flour bags, she was always thinking. If she was not planning and organizing the next project she would work on, she was thinking about her deceased hus-band, Utli, and her three grown children. She and Utli had had a marriage that was "in the old-custom way." Her mother, Ekiyuq, arranged the marriage with people from the village of Seelvik, which wasn't far from a big lake where people fished for sheefish.

During their short time together, Utli had shared his life stories with her. Once he told her what it was like when he was a boy. He and some other boys his age were permitted to enter the *qasgi*, where only men were allowed. He told Sikki about being scared because it was not like being in his own house. The boys were about eight, nine, and ten years old. He knew who everyone was from being around the village. But in the *qasgi*, the adults seemed to change. In that place, everyone was so important. They were important because each adult male was an expert in something. Sometimes, there were two or three experts on using a specific tool. But in the end, they always took the advice of the oldest expert. The elders lived life the longest. There was no question whose advice should be listened to when an elder had proved his skills.

As Sikki worked on her net, she thought of a particular time when Utli talked to her about his teacher Mungnuk. Mungnuk had been chief of a village when he was a young man. He had been a good hunter and a natural leader, first with his hunting crew and then in his village. With all that experience behind him, now he was a great teacher, not only for his expertise in making harpoon points, but also for his storytelling. She recalled Utli's story that she loved to listen to, about three strong giants.

At Ipnatchiaq River, there was a village. People lived there for the winter, in subterranean dwellings. This particular year, people were dying from the flu. Their dwellings had daylight from the roof. An opening was covered by beluga intestines sewn together to make a translucent window.

In this village lived a family. The father was a very tall man. His wife was a normal-sized person. For the man to live in their house, they built a huge place. The logs were slanted and laid on a frame side by side. The house was discovered in later years, and people knew who lived in this huge dwelling because stories were told of this family.

The couple had three sons. They were six, eight, and ten years old when their father died from the flu. At this time, people were very afraid of death. When a person died, the custom was to leave the family alone, and so no one helped them.

The village people heard that the man had died in his big subterranean home. Even though the dwelling was big, the entrance was small to keep the warmth inside. The widow and her three sons needed to get the tall man out of the house, and so they tied a rope around him. They used a thick length of braided rawhide called an *aleq*. Not even the relatives helped because they did not want to become infected with the flu.

The mother and her sons wanted to pull him up through the window at the top of the dwelling, so she climbed up to pull the window open. The dead man was so huge that they tried many times, and each time his shoulders would get stuck in the window. The three boys were not strong enough to really help their mother. The father would slip back down to the floor. It was a sad time; everyone cried. After trying many times, they just gave up and left him inside the big house. They took what was theirs and moved on to find another place to live.

In those days, because of superstition, the family had to get rid of the belongings of the deceased. When the family couldn't accomplish this task and no one would help them, the three sons became resentful toward people. As they grew up, they became cruel people. They never forgot how poor they were, and they became revengeful toward people who wouldn't help them. As adults, the three brothers were huge people. They were like giants and very strong.

The mother understood why her relatives wouldn't assist her family. She tried to help her boys understand, but they wouldn't listen to her. Illiganeq, one of the sons, was not only cruel, but he would do horrible things to people, over and over again, to make them suffer.

Finally, their mother sent one son way up north. His name was Kuvravaq, which means "big net." The place he moved to was called Tikiqaq. When he arrived there, he found a big lake back in the mountains. And in that lake lived a huge mouse called *ugrunukpuk,* which means "smaller than a mouse with a pointed nose." (In real life, *ugrunuks* are voles, and they are smaller than a regular mouse. But when you put *puk* at the end of a word, it means that something is very big.) People who lived there would tell the people not to ride a *kayaq* in that lake or else the *ugrunukpuk* would get that person, *kayaq* and all.

The other son, Suluq, was sent to the Qigiqtaq area. He often came back to visit his brother Illiganeq, who stayed close to home. On these visits, they would scheme to get even with the people. Whenever a chance came, they would pick on people and make them do things for them because they were bigger and stronger.

One day, Suluq decided to get rid of Illiganeq. He thought that Illiganeq must be giving their mother grief since he was living close to her. Their mother lived with the other village people, at a place where there was a gigantic bluff called Kippalu. By the bluff, there was a monstrous boulder in the water. The lower part of the monstrous boulder was smaller than the top part. But it was the same height as the bluff next to it. It had no name. It was just a big rock coming out of the water.

Suluq said to Illiganeq, "Let's use the *aleq* (sealskin rawhide rope) to lasso the top of that big boulder." It wasn't very close, but they agreed to try. "Let's do it!" Suluq still had his mind made up about getting rid of Illiganeq.

So on a certain day, they went to the boulder, determined to lasso it. They would lasso the boulder and then tie the *aleq* to the mainland on the bluff. The plan was to get the *aleq* tight and then walk on it and hang from it. To decide who would go first, they drew sticks.

Illiganeq won the first draw. He was excited to go first because he wanted to walk the tight *aleq* to the boulder. He was a strong but agile man, and he made it across.

While Suluq was still on the mainland, he yelled across to Illiganeq. "Brother, you are so cruel. Why don't you throw yourself down from the cliff!" Then he immediately cut the *aleq*.

When the *aleq* was cut, over 200 feet of it dangled down the steep boulder from Illiganeq, reaching all the way to the water. He quickly pulled the *aleq* up and tied it around his waist. Then he dove headfirst into the water below, which was very deep. The people called the bluff "Kippalu" for that reason. After making this dive, he managed to come back up from the deep water alive. He made no plans to get even with his brother.

Suluq returned to his home. After that incident, Illiganeq made a home at Chamisso Island, which was really a set of islands, and he chose the last island. Because he was a great hunter who could provide well, he began a family, starting with one wife and ending up with three wives.

Illiganeq spent lots of time on top of the island watching for animals that he could harvest for a winter food supply. To keep his *aleq* damp, he carved a vessel in a big rock and filled it with water. In it, he soaked the *aleq*, to keep it pliable. That way, he was always ready to go after animals to provide food for his three families.

His first wife was a good woman who made a home for him and his other two wives. Despite that, Illiganeq was still a very cruel man. Whenever one of his wives had a baby, he let it live if it was a girl, because he wanted them to be his slaves when they got older. When the wives had baby boys, he killed them. In spite of all his cruelty, his wives made him feel like a big chief. He behaved like he was one.

One day, his brother Kuvravaq from Tikiqaq invited him to go on a "grand hunt" as he described it. He told him to come up with a *kayaq* and his hunting gear. So Illiganeq accepted the invitation and got himself ready with a *kayaq*, and for this hunt he also took a big harpoon with a flint tip.

Illiganeq traveled north to meet up with his brother Kuvravaq. Before they started out, they planned how they would hunt *ugrunukpuk*, the huge mouse. Illiganeq had huge lungs. He could stay underwater as long as a bearded seal. So he told his brother he would go down in the water and hold the *ugrunukpuk* by the tail so his brother could harpoon and puncture it as many times as he could. When they sighted the *ugrunukpuk*, they hunted according to their plan.

Because the animal was so strong, the brothers worked very hard at killing it. No one knows how long it took to kill the giant mouse. When it finally died, they pulled it up to the surface of the water and onto the shore. After they skinned the animal and cut it up, they could both stand up together in the skull. The creature was that huge. After they had killed the *ugrunukpuk*, the people were able to hunt at that lake. The two brothers became heroes.

Illiganeq then returned home. It was spring-time, and at that time of year, he liked to go across the bay so that he could travel up and down the Kaniq River. He told his wives that it was time for him to hunt caribou. His method of transportation was to swim across the bay.

This day, as he was crossing the bay, he met a school of smelt. Smelt are a fish without slime. The fish were many and they stuck to his hairy body. He was so heavy with the fish that he sank down to the bottom of the bay. He managed to free himself from the smelt because he was able to hold his breath as long as an *ugruk*.

When he began his caribou hunt, he waited behind a big bluff. After a few days, he spotted the herd coming. Because he was so huge, it was easy for him to herd the caribou. He drove them down the beach and toward the area under the bluff. Taking out his sling, he picked up rocks to use as bullets. Then he went up on the bluff and used his sling to kill the caribou.

He worked quickly and skillfully with the sling. He knew how many animals he needed to feed his big family. When he got enough for this trip, like in the past, he tied them together with his *aleq* and swam back home across the bay, pulling the raft of caribou behind him.

In the area where this story took place, the bluff was a landmark. We remember it to this day. People were afraid to go there. Every time people had to travel that way in their *umiaqs*, they would stop and pull up on shore instead of sailing around the bluff. The bluff is called Toeahleveq.

Just off Toeahleveq, a gigantic water creature lived. It is said that there were some people who did not listen and would not take orders from the wise elders. They tried to paddle their *umiaqs* as fast as they could, but they found they could not compete with that animal. It was called *amitshuq,* which means "walrus skin covering for an *umiaq.*" The animal would grab the whole boat and take it down under the water. It looked like a giant octopus.

One day, Illiganeq decided to kill the animal. This time, his brother would not be there, so he had to carry out the task by himself. With his *aleq* and his sharpened harpoon in his mouth, he swam toward the point called Toeahleveq. The gigantic water creature quickly came up to him and pulled him down in the sea. Illiganeq knew what he must do to survive. He cut around the creature's round head over and over again with his sharp harpoon. Eventually, the *amitshuq*'s grip began to loosen on him. And he again got rid of a monster that was killing the people.

One day, one of Illiganeq's three wives gave birth to a baby boy, and Illiganeq again demanded that it die. The next time he went hunting, the wives schemed to let the baby boy live. All the wives and all his daughters got lots of pegs ready. It was fall and the ground was not yet frozen.

The wives sang a shaman chant when he came home. They fed him big helpings of caribou soup. That type of singing put him to sleep using the power of evil spirits. When he was asleep, they tied him up with his own *aleq* as hard as they could. Then they used the pegs to pin him to the ground. The wife who had just given birth to the baby boy picked up the harpoon and plunged it into Illiganeq's gigantic body.

So it does not pay to be cruel, even if you are a big, strong giant.

Sikki then thought of her three grown children. When they were born, she and Utli, her husband, gave them Inupiat names: Ekiyuq, Ahkavluk, and Kitiruaq. They were later given the English names Topsy, Dick, and Ruby. The three children were young when their father died, and Sikki had worked very hard so that they could stay together. She worked so hard that it was unnecessary for her to have another husband. She was able to feed and clothe herself and the children, because she was an excellent seamstress and could sew any item of clothing. Now two of them were living in other villages and one was raising her own family.

Topsy, the oldest, got married to a white man whose last name was Swanson. She was busy taking care of her own family. But Sikki knew that Topsy would come to help her, if she needed it. Sikki had her own sod house and it was warm. She knew all the village people and they treated her well, and she in turn always tried to help them. In the spring, she and her Storyteller friends worked together to put up the *ugruk* meat caught by the hunters. Throughout the year, they did all kinds of gathering and preparation activities together to put up food for the winter.

Sikki's son Dick and her daughter Ruby were living up the Kobuk River. Sikki had traveled there to try to convince her daughter Ruby to move back to Ipnatchiaq, but she wouldn't. Ruby allowed Sikki to bring back her grandson Emuk to live with her; he was two at the time. It was 1921. Ruby was in a relationship with a man whose name was Murphy Eterorock. (Missionaries later changed his last name to Johnson.) And Dick, her son, was still single, and had gotten used to living along the river.

Sikki thought about her grandson Emuk, who had lived with her for four years and was now six. He now attended school at the big wood schoolhouse in their village. His name had been changed to Walter when he went to school. His teacher, Tony Joule, was a Native man from the Qikiqtaġruk area. The idea of going to school to learn something was so different from traditional ways. Sikki had learned everything about life from her mother and her mother's friends and relatives. But now, they say, children have to go to school. So she took care of her grandson and walked him to school, but she never went inside. There was no need for her to go inside.

When Sikki had brought Walter back with her to Ipnatchiaq, she began sewing a sleeping bag for him out of reindeer skins. She had worked for the reindeer skins by helping the owners of a herd when they needed help corralling the animals. Every chance she got, she did all kinds of work, since she no longer had a husband to help her. It took her a long time to scrape the reindeer hides. And then it took longer to wring the skins to soften and cure them. Now Walter had his own reindeer skin sleeping bag. When he came to live with her, she also sewed him a parka of squirrel skins. She had set traps to catch the squirrels the previous spring. At that time, she didn't know the skins would be used for Walter's parka.

In the springtime, Sikki and her Storyteller friends went out and trapped squirrels. That's the way it was. Squirrel skins made great parkas, not only because they were warm but because the parkas were reversible. When it was cold, the fur could be worn on the inside, and when it got warmer, the fur was worn on the outside. Walter loved his parka. At school, he wore the fur on the outside.

When Walter wasn't in school, he loved to go hunting with Sikki. She showed him how to make snares to catch ptarmigan. He loved to walk with her across the river to the willows where she would find the ptarmigan. They would look for tracks in the snow. He watched how she would bend a little willow down to the ground, so when a ptarmigan stepped in the loop of the snare, the willow would snap back up and the ptarmigan would be caught.

Walter learned to wring the ptarmigan's neck, just as Sikki did. When it was time to pluck the feathers from the bird, he got excited. The ptarmigan has a balloon down the esophagus where it stores its food. It is slimy and wet, but after touching many of them, you get used to it. Walter loved to inflate the balloons, and Sikki would then tie them with sinew. One winter, Walter had over two dozen balloons hanging up. And they both loved to eat the ptarmigan. The meat was tender and the broth was delicious.

In Utli's time, there was a *qasgi* where young boys were taught how to hunt. Now there wasn't a *qasgi* anymore. Sikki worried about that. She knew her grandson needed someone to teach him how to hunt like the men hunted. She was teaching him all she knew, but that was just hunting small game, like snaring ptarmigan and trapping red fox to barter at Magid's store. Sikki knew that she should find someone to take Walter out on the ice in the springtime to hunt bearded seal. That experience would be very important because bearded seal sustained the whole village year-round. Also, he would need to learn to care for and use a dog team, to cross the bay and to hunt caribou. The caribou herd didn't travel near their village.

Sikki made up her mind that she was going to ask her neighbor, whose English name was Emily Barr, to take care of Walter if anything happened to her. Just in case his mother Ruby was still up north. Maybe one of Emily's daughter's families could adopt Walter. He was getting to the age when he should be taught all these things.

Sikki tried to teach Walter everything she could, and to keep him learning. She was happy when, last fall, he watched the men set the seal nets in the ocean along with almost the whole village. He was playing with other little boys his age, but every time she looked at him, she reminded him to watch. She didn't know if he understood when she told him that someday, he would inherit a seal net spot from someone.

She remembered that Walter and two other little boys had been skipping rocks into the ocean. It was a calm day and she could see they were having fun. At the same time, the villagers began to catch seals caught in their nets. Eventually, someone gathered driftwood to make a bonfire on the beach. The weather was getting cold and the hot fire felt good.

When Kiloweluq, Sikki's relative, said he was going out to set his part of the net, she called Walter over to watch with her. Kiloweluq's net was the third one out, so it had to be set between two other nets. At the end of each net, a heavy rock was placed so that the net would stay in place. The men would go to the bluff to locate a rock that was big enough to weigh down a net. When the time came for each person to drop the rock, it was placed on top of the *kayaq* along with the net that was made of sealskin. The skins of some of the seals that were being caught would also be made into a net.

As Sikki and Walter watched, he said he wished he could go out in the *kayaq*. She said he would be doing that soon enough. But now he should watch how Kiloweluq, the old man, paddled his *kayaq* so it would go forward and backward. And she noticed that Kiloweluq had his raingear on. She hoped that after all the work was done and because there were people around, she could coax him into giving them a little show by doing a rollover in the water in his *kayaq*. When one person started, Sikki knew it would turn into a competition.

Every year, among the men who were setting their seal nets, a rollover competition developed. They started with one rollover, and if everyone made it, then they would try two rollovers in a row, and the number kept going up. Sakapuk and his wife Ayi, or Ayichak, had their net place right off shore. Then Aviniq was second, Kiloweluq was third, Ahniyaq was fourth, and the last net setter was Kavaruq. All of them were skilled at handling their hunting gear and especially their *kayaqs*. During all those years of setting seal nets, all of them had been winners of the rollover competition one year or another. All the Ipnatchiaq people would gather on the beach, and the atmosphere would be loud with talking, laughter, and children screeching.

When someone noticed movement in a seal net, the competition stopped long enough for each hunter to go out to check his net. When Sikki's relative Kiloweluq got a seal in the net, he pulled up the net and speared it. Then after pulling his *kayaq* halfway up on the beach, he motioned for Sikki to bring him a ladle of fresh water, a gesture of respect for the animal that would feed them. It was believed that the animal should have a last drink so that its spirit could spread the message that it was good to feed these people.

It was as if she had planned it. Sikki heard her grandson outside, and she was at a good place to stop working on her net. School was over for the day. After school, Walter would come home, have a little snack that was usually a hard cracker with some butter on it and maybe canned milk mixed with warm water and sugar.

Today, Sikki would have him help her sort through some roots of the *muminuq*, or spruce tree. The roots would be used as floats for the net she was working on. Each piece of root would be inspected for weakness. It needed to be solid and strong so that when a hole was drilled in it, it wouldn't break apart. Then Walter would be sent on an errand to borrow a drill. She had already arranged with her neighbor, an old miner, to borrow his drill.

A long time ago in the spring, the miner wanted to pick the mushrooms on the roof of her little sod house. Sikki didn't eat mushrooms because the people did not eat them. The old miner loved those mushrooms and he knew how to cook them. This miner continued to live in the village year-round, whereas most miners packed up and left before freezeup. She had seen him use the drill when he was building his little house made of lumber. And he had told her she was more than welcome to borrow the drill whenever she needed it. He had access to some lumber because he worked about twenty miles upriver at the gold mine. The white people up there built houses with lumber.

3

Qutla

The following morning when Sikki was by herself again and the routine chores were done, she laid out the net she was making by the *aleq* and the floats she and Walter had made from the roots of the *muminuq* tree. Today I'm happy because I can see that the floats we made will work, she said to herself. I chose a root that was not rotten, and the weather conditions dried it out good after it floated here from flooded rivers somewhere. *Taqu* (thank you), she said.

Maybe the root came from the Kaniq River where my cousin Qutla is from, Sikki thought. I didn't want to dwell on sad things today, but here I am again thinking of her. To put some things to rest, I guess I must make myself go through this, Sikki told herself. I thought about sharing her story with my friends, but first I need to remember the things she told me in order to decide whether they would help someone's life. Maybe her story will teach our children, and especially my grandson Walter, to obey and to begin to learn the meaning of humility.

And so Sikki remembered her cousin Qutla's story.

At one time, Qutla's stepfather, Mungnuk, became sick. He was a shaman and the people respected him. The family called another shaman to make him well. That shaman admonished the family not to braid their hair, or grass, or anything. Qutla told me that they all understood what that meant, because her mother sometimes braided her hair after it was oiled with caribou marrow. But being just a small child, Qutla forgot what the shaman told them.

It was common for the children to play outside with other children. All the world was their playground. On this day, Qutla and her friends were playing with the long grass that grew everywhere in the summer. They were playing "Mommy" and pretending to braid the grass like their mothers braided their hair. Only after she made a few braiding motions and saw the grass taking on a braid shape did she remember she was not supposed to braid anything. She stood up and looked toward the *qasgi* where her father was. He soon died.

Sikki remembered the many happy times she and her cousin had at the shelter by the ocean, gathering clay for pots. The braid incident must have happened after that, she thought, because they never went back there again.

The people in the village all began to shun Qutla. Her own mother, Paneluq, told her, "You have Mungnuk's breath. You are the one who should not be here."

Sikki could not imagine her mother telling her that she should have been the one to die. Paneluq had been enjoying her life being married to an important man. She had all the food and all the skins to have her family's clothes made. Mungnuk was a great hunter and helped the whole village. She had a taste of what it was like to be with someone the people respected. When he died, her situation changed. Everything that was accumulated by Mungnuk and Paneluq went to his family, and that made Paneluq poor.

I wonder who was important enough to have made that rule, Sikki thought. The rule was probably made by a powerful shaman, and the people were afraid to go against his or her wishes. Maybe the rule was made by a shaman who would have profited from the death of a son. It was a rule that was most devastating for a widow and her children.

Qutla was treated as the lowliest creature. She believed it would have been better if she had starved to death. She kept herself alive by eating scraps from other peoples' meals. Her own mother not only regarded her with scorn, but allowed her just enough food so she didn't die. Because Qutla had no way to keep herself clean, she became covered with sores and began to smell bad, and most of her hair fell out.

Sikki remembered Qutla telling her that she understood why she was being mistreated. She had caused her stepfather to die by disobeying. But she had loved him very much. He had cared for her like she was his own daughter, making sure that she had caribou marrow to keep her hair shiny. It was only when Paneluq forced her to live with Mungnuk's family, since they had all their belongings, that Qutla was offered some compassion.

A young woman in the household began to sneak her a little food. One day, she brought some caribou bone marrow. The young woman and Qutla ate some of the marrow and then they oiled their hair with the rest. When a woman noticed the two girls, she said with scorn, "The poor fatherless one is oiling her hair."

Although Qutla was an outcast, she still had normal feelings. So when she heard what that woman said, she was hurt and angry, and wanted to get back at her by hoping that something bad would happen to her. Years later, the person who had made the unkind comment had a daughter who became sick and lost all of her hair. Sikki recalled, Qutla told me she regretted having had those vengeful thoughts. She taught me that you need to be careful what you say and do, because if you create grief for others, it will come back to you.

Qutla spent about two or three years with Mungnuk's family. But her life did not get any easier. "Who will help me, when my mother, Paneluq, hates me and forces me to beg from this family," Qutla said to me.

Every time someone treated Qutla inhumanely, she thought, "What could be worse than this?" But the next incident would be even worse. She was an outcast. To be shunned, in their culture, made others want to follow the rules very closely, and Qutla was made the scapegoat.

Despite the cruelties to her, she somehow kept her sense of humanity. When she was twelve or thirteen, she considered committing suicide, but she could not when she remembered the love of her younger sister.

When Qutla became Egaq's wife, he would chase her out of their humble home. After that had happened many times, she tried to kill herself by making a rope out of her clothes. But when she hung herself, the rope didn't hold her because her clothes were too rotten. Then she thought of using a knife to cut her throat, but she stopped. "My sister Nuyaqik would be sad if I ended my life," Qutla realized.

Sikki shut her eyes and cried for her cousin and lifetime friend. Then she told herself, I need to stop my mind from remembering Qutla's story for a while.

So she put down her net, got up, put on her parka, and went outside. There she sat down and watched for any activity that would distract her, whether it was someone going upriver to get ice or people going out to set ptarmigan snares. Sikki sat there outside her house for a long time.

When she went back inside to her net making, she found herself thinking about her cousin again.

How could Qutla have gone through the next two traumatizing events with Egaq without taking her own life? Sikki wondered.

Qutla felt a ray of hope that Egaq would finally accept her. But when she woke up one morning, she found that he and his brother and mother, Augrotuq, had left her. They left all her things and so she knew they had deserted her. Later she discovered they had left so Egaq could find another wife.

Qutla then found her uncle's family, and they allowed her to live with them. But Egaq's next wife rejected him, so he and his family returned. Egaq forced Qutla to be his wife again, although she did not want him back. While she was with Egaq, her uncle's family deserted her. Augrotuq woke Qutla one morning and told her what was going on, and Qutla ran outside and along the shore after their boat.

As she was chasing the boat, she found a friend of her mother's who comforted her, and took her to the spot where her uncle's family made camp. They refused to take her in, and another family accepted her. But since they were not related, they did not defend her when Egaq came and took her away again.

Ironically, Qutla felt comforted when she had to go through the traditional rites of becoming a woman. She felt less alone, because every young woman went through the same ritual. First she was put out of the camp with no blankets. And she had to wear a veil over her whole face that was made of seal intestines with slits for her eyes. She could see out, but no one could see her face. Her husband felt that if he stayed near her, he would be killed by evil spirits. So she had to move about a quarter of a mile away. She lived under a tree with no protection except the fur clothes she had on. Once in a while, Augrotuq would throw her some food like she was a dog. Everyone stayed away from her, afraid of the evil spirits.

Soon, Egaq's people needed to travel up the Seelvik River. If a girl at that stage of her life waded in water, she would be eaten by worms and then sores would overtake her body. When they came to a creek, Augrotuq said, "I will pack you across."

After that, Qutla felt sorry for Augrotuq because she was uneasy touching her. So Qutla said, "After we go across, take off your parka and beat on it, to shake off my essence." And when Augrotuq did that, Qutla felt better. For the first time in her life, someone had taken her advice, and strangely enough, that made her feel like she was part of the family.

Finally, one day, she sensed that the family was starting to take care of her. Her first baby was born by a campfire. Soon after, she carried her baby to a snow hut where she had to stay since it was a girl baby. The superstition dictated that she must remain in the snow hut for five days without food, water, or heat. People were really afraid of evil spirits and would not help her.

While she remained there, Egaq moved across the river. It was at this time that Qutla's own mother, Paneluq, and her sister Nuyaqik moved near her. When Qutla could move back to her house, she discovered that there were no blankets because Egaq had taken everything.

Qutla's baby died and Egaq sent word that he wasn't coming back. So, ten days after giving birth and losing her baby, she was out setting snares for ptarmigan. This activity caused her great suffering. It was the custom to throw away all your clothing after having a new baby. But Qutla had no new clothes to wear, so she had to keep her old clothes.

Paneluq went to Augrotuq to beg for food, and sometimes she gave her some. One time she also brought back news that Egaq was looking for a new wife again.

About four months later, Paneluq began praying to her dead husband's spirit because she was becoming weak from lack of food. Qutla pitied her mother, and so she went to Egaq, walking where there was no trail so Egaq would not walk in her footsteps and die. And when she found Egaq, she asked, "Could you love me and take care of me? If you don't, I will starve to death, and you will be at fault because I became weak bearing your child."

Egaq answered, "Yes, I will love you. We are traveling to the coast to hunt seals, and you may follow."

Just those words gave Qutla hope. Qutla, Paneluq, and Nuyaqik followed Egaq's family, staying a good distance behind. They built a sled to use for their journey, and they had a grass mat blanket, a caribou skin, and a seal poke.

On the way to the coast, they carved out a snow shelter and set ptarmigan snares, and they had caught ptarmigan by the next morning. After traveling the next day, they found a small dugout house where they remained for many stormy days. Augrotuq began to bring them food.

One morning, Egaq came to their dugout house and threw them a frozen fish. As Qutla waited for the fish to thaw, she thought about how Egaq and his family were probably already far away, since they had a sail on their sled.

The three women set out again, pulling their own sled. They traveled all day without food, and it was so cold Qutla thought she would die. That night, when they saw Egaq's camp ahead, they dug a shelter in the snow.

The next morning, Augrotuq brought them seal oil and fish. She also brought a seal poke so Qutla could make Egaq some *mukluks*. Qutla was so hungry she ate some of the seal poke with the hair still on it. When her sister caught two rabbits, by custom Qutla was not allowed to eat the rabbit meat because it had not yet been a year since her baby died.

One day, they met a person who told them that the people were catching a lot of fish near Qikiqtaġruk. When they arrived there, they finally ate a good meal of cooked fish. Wherever the three women traveled, they would snare ptarmigan.

They began to feel sorry for Egaq because he was not catching any seals and he was getting poor. But he was still afraid of evil spirits, so he would not eat any of the food they gave him.

Near Qikiqtaġruk, it was always stormy. While they were there, a traveler told them the people were catching fish at Nelson Point. So they packed their bedding and walked there. When they reached the point, one of Qutla's cousins welcomed them, and proclaimed to Paneluq, "You and your daughters will live now!"

Since Qutla still wore her old, ragged clothes, Egaq left her again when his family went back to their boat. Egaq and Augrotuq still would not eat with her. Paneluq talked to Qutla and advised her to follow them once again. When they followed Egaq and his family, it was as before.

Finally, when she caught up with them, Egaq said, "If you make new clothes, then you may come and live with us." And for a few years, he was true to her.

When Sikki got tired of weaving her net, she told herself, I must stop remembering my cousin's story for now. It makes me sad and tired. I don't want to be sad when my grandson comes home.

So once again Sikki got up, put some wood in the stove, and went outside. She sat down in the same place and waited for her grandson to come home.

When Walter arrived, he said, "Hi grandma," with a big smile.

4

Village Recipes

Although the Storytellers were going to meet at her home again, Sikki decided that she would ask each one to tell her own story. They decided to meet two times a month while the days were dark. They knew it made them happier and enhanced their sense of purpose in their lives, which was first to help their own families and second to help others in the village.

Throughout the years, they had helped one another mostly by putting food away for the winter. And they were all midwives because they had had their children in the old way—by themselves. But nowadays, women didn't labor in childbirth by themselves. So each of them was called by the other's family at one time or another to help deliver babies.

Changes were taking place in the village since the gold miners had started arriving every summer. In the old days, they didn't have a trading post, and now there was one called Magid's store. Some houses were now built from lumber instead of sod like the one Sikki lived in. She knew if she still had a husband to help her, she'd probably have a house made of lumber too. But she liked her sod home. It was solid and warm, and her friends liked coming over to visit.

Today, since they were arriving in the middle of the day, she would serve them ptarmigan soup. She knew she would probably talk about last weekend, when she took her grandson along with her to catch ptarmigan. They had caught enough ptarmigan for the whole week. Sikki would ask her friends if they wanted to take some home. In fact, they had decided that today, they would be sharing recipes and sharing something about themselves.

Sikki had just enough wooden bowls and spoons to serve soup to her friends. Some of the bowls she had were from when she and Utli became man and wife in the old way. He was good at carving bowls out of birch wood. She still had a few large bowls and two big platters they had served their food on. Gradually, each of the bowls was used to serve one kind of food. One bowl was used to serve ptarmigan in winter and duck in summer. Another was used for bearded seal or seal meat and blubber. One of the platters was used to serve fish. On her shopping trips to Magid's store, she noticed tin bowls. Sikki told herself that she would trap more red fox and get herself some tin bowls like the tin cups.

When the Storytellers were seated together, Uto always sat closest to Sikki on her left. The Storytellers were creatures of habit, always sitting in the same spot at their sessions. And they went clockwise when they spoke.

Uto looked as if she were the wife of a giant. Her high cheek bones gave her a distinguished look. Although her eyes were narrow, they were long and sheltered by a strong forehead. And her nose gave her a striking profile. It wasn't short and stubby like most of the people's noses. The people believed that they didn't have a big, long nose because it might freeze. But Uto's nose was long, and she looked like she could be the wife of an important person.

When she started to give her recipe, Uto smiled and acknowledged each of them. There was an air about her that made her friends envious, and they showed this by teasing her. They would sometimes ask her which of the three strong giants in Utli's story she was married to. Was she the first wife or second wife? And again, as she started, one of the Storytellers asked, "Could you have chosen which giant you would have for your husband?" Who couldn't help but laugh! These Storytellers loved to laugh and especially laugh with each other.

By now, everyone had her piece of brown wrapping paper from Magid's store. Everyone had an indelible pencil, and each wet the lead with the saliva from her mouth. Uto began by drawing herself and her husband.

"My husband was also from Ipnatchiaq, like I am," Uto told them. "Our parents arranged an old-style marriage. When we started to be man and wife, we lived in a sod house on the west side of the village." Then Uto drew a long beach line from east to west. Next she drew their little sod house with a window made of beluga intestines at the top.

"As the years went by," she continued, "the white miners and missionaries began to arrive, and the

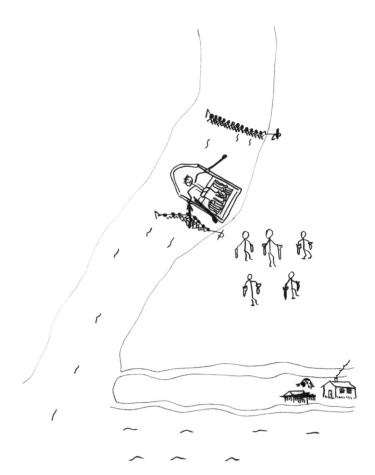

Uto's Picture-Writing: *Fishing on the Ipnatchiaq River*
[DRAWING BY LORETTA OUTWATER COX]

people started building houses made of lumber. We then moved into a wood house built for Miss Stratton, the missionary, and we used our sod house as a winter storage place for our supplies. Uto drew a little house made of lumber with two glass windows and a stovepipe at the top.

She told her Storyteller friends, "I have truly marveled at the difference a glass window makes." And as she looked at Sikki's one glass window and at Sikki, she said, "Sikki, you must feel the same way about your window." And all agreed by nodding their heads.

As she was nodding, Uto wet her pencil and all of them wet their pencils. "Now draw the Ipnatchiaq River which goes from north to south," Uto told them. "Now draw a set net about a half a mile up the river," she said. As they were all drawing the set net, she drew a number of floats in the water and drew a little wave near the floats.

"Now draw a little boat with one person in it," she said. "That is my husband checking the net. Now draw a fish that he is trying to untangle from the net. Then draw ten fish, because that is the number of fish we often catch when they are running. Lay them on top of each other in the boat."

Uto hesitated while her friends, the Storytellers, caught up with her. She looked like a teacher checking her students and had a big smile. All of them knew it was quicker to carry the fish home from upriver than to bring them down in the little boat, because someone would have to row the boat back up. So Uto said to draw five people, each carrying two fish back to their house on the west side of the village.

Then Uto told them, "Draw a fish cache near my house made of lumber. It is located on the ocean side."

Then she told them, "Draw ten fish hanging over the pole in the cache, and draw them with the skin on the outside because we dry them first with the skin side out. After one day, my family turns the fish over to dry the meaty side.

"Today my recipe will be making half-dried boiled salmon," Uto told her friends. "After the salmon has dried for three days, take down enough for a meal, and cut it into three-inch pieces. Put the pieces in boiling water. Let the half-dried fish boil until the raw part of the fish is done. Serve it on your fish platter with a side dish of greens and seal oil. That is my recipe."

~~~~~~~

Panea knew that it would be her turn after Uto. To the Storytellers, she was known to first say a Bible verse. Today her Bible verse was John 3:16.

Instead of saying it in English, Panea was learning to say the verses in Inupiaq. She had started studying the Bible while they were living across the bay and up the river.

In Inupiaq, Panea said, "For God so loved the world, he gave his only begotten son, that whosoever believeth in him shall have everlasting life."

Panea then told the Storytellers, "Draw four little rectangles and an *ulu*."

And she continued, "I have made this dish so many times that I can now cut caribou fat so fast that my husband, who is Japanese, said I remind him of the cooks in his homeland who chop vegetables very fast."

Then she told them, "Draw a bowl with the chopped fat in it, and draw a hand by the bowl to signify that the hand should mix the fat around in the bowl.

"Now, let's draw something that's hard to draw," she continued. "It's a seal poke. We all keep our seal oil in a seal poke, so let's have a contest to see who can draw a seal poke the best. Sikki will be the judge."

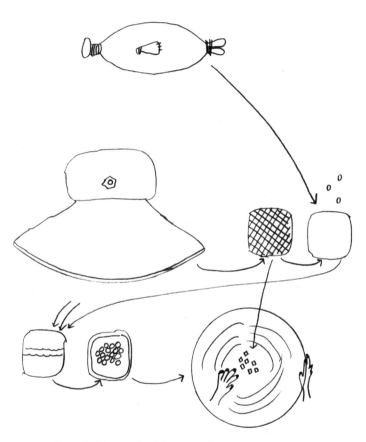

Panea's Picture-Writing: *Caribou Fat, Bowl, Ulu, and Seal Poke* [DRAWING BY LORETTA OUTWATER COX]

It was quiet as they drew.

Then Panea said, "Whoever wins will bring a bowl of *akutuq*, or Eskimo ice cream, home for her family tonight."

While the Storytellers drew a seal poke, Sikki checked the stove. She went outside to get more wood and noticed the weather was getting stormy. But they were used to that. On the coast, it was always windy and stormy in the wintertime. In fact, she was grateful for the wind. At times, the sound of the wind kept her company, especially after her husband had passed on. Sikki told herself, I love the sound of the wind.

When Sikki went back in, the Storytellers were still quietly drawing a seal poke. She filled the kettle with water to make more tea. No one was in a hurry, and they knew which two Storytellers were the artists. They all were excellent skin sewers because they made all their families' clothes. But two of them added an extra something to their sewing because they were gifted artists. The contest would be between Ayi and Nupa.

It was finally time to judge. Panea said, "Time is up."

Everyone knew it was time for a break, so they went outside. Sikki said, "While you are on break, I'll review the pictures and tell you who the winner is when you come back inside."

When they were all seated again, Panea asked Sikki to let them know who the winner was.

Sikki said to the others, "In our lives, we have worked so hard to put food away that we mostly help each other instead of competing with each other. It's always been okay to compete in the Eskimo games when we do celebrate. It is okay because that's when competition is accepted by everyone. But to compete in a drawing contest is a new concept for us. Maybe that's what the white people do, and they are coming to our village every spring now."

Sikki asked each one of them by name, "Do you think it is a good thing to do this?" The Storytellers agreed that competition is okay if it is sanctioned by the whole group. Otherwise, competition could cause friction and jealousy.

Once Sikki knew that all agreed to the competition, she announced that the winner was Nupa. And Ayi was the second winner. "Both will be taking some *agupuk* home today," she said.

Ayi knew that she was going to speak next. "According to Sikki, I'm not supposed to be jealous of Nupa," she said. As she looked everyone in the eye, she told them, "I won't be, only a little!" She seemed pleased with herself that she had made everyone laugh.

"I'm going to give you the names of my husband and children in English first," she said. "I'd like to start there because I've been practicing the names since the missionaries, Martha Hunnicutt, Anna and Edward Foster, and Martha Hadley, gave them names after 1899 when the Qikiqtaġruk Friends Church was established on October 22 of that year." And with that introduction, she began.

"My oldest son's name is Thomas," said Ayi. "Then the second child is a girl, who was given the name Martha. Archie is the third child, and the baby is Gladys. And I love my husband's name the most because it is easy to say. His name is Sam." When she paused, the Storytellers clapped.

When Ayi started to speak in Inupiaq again, she was very animated. She was known as one who loved to talk. All her Storyteller friends enjoyed watching her because she had the marks of beauty on her chin. Ayi was the last person in their village to have old-style tattoos. At other times when they visited, she had told them what she remembered about when the tattoos

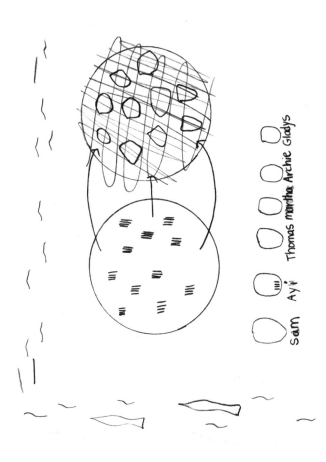

Ayi's Picture-Writing: *Ayi's Family, and Aged Salmon Heads* [Drawings by Loretta Outwater Cox]

were put on her chin. It was a slow process done with black soot. "And it hurt so bad," she said, "but it was a ritual to please the spirits so I would have a good life." All of them thought of that as they listened to her now.

Ayi was proud of her children and their new English names, and she began drawing each of them, from oldest to youngest. Then she drew herself with the tattoos on her chin. Then she drew her husband, Sam.

"He is a tall man," Ayi told them. As she was drawing him, she talked proudly about how he had won the *kayaq* rollover contest last fall at the setting of the seal nets. She said to her friends, "It is our belief never to boast about ourselves. My husband didn't boast when he won the *kayaq* contest, but I can boast for him," she said, laughing.

Ayi continued. "Before I give my recipe for making aged salmon heads, I want to mention that I am related to a woman named Qutuq. Her family used to travel by boat after breakup to Qikiqtaġruk to go to the trade fair. My family and Qutuq's family would live side by side in tents on the beach while that was going on. We knew we were related because our parents called each other cousins. When the trade fair was over, Qutuq's family would travel down to Ipnatchiaq with us. But after a couple days of rest, they started their long journey to Chaqtuliq. They would always say that they would stop at different villages for a few days to fish and dry salmon and to pick berries, as these activities would be going on as they passed by.

Then Ayi began to describe her recipe. "My recipe requires a whole river and a little creek. So I brought some material that we can use in our picture-writing to make the river and the little creek. I also brought some red leaves that I picked before the snow came, and those will be the fish in the river and then the fish heads.

"Okay, now let's tear a strip from the end of your paper," Ayi instructed. "Make it a little wider than the second strip we will tear."

When everyone had torn two pieces of paper, Ayi pulled out a small container from her bag. "I made this mixture this morning. It is gray charcoal mixed with water. Everyone take some and rub it on the piece of paper that is the river and then on the piece that is the little creek. By the way, the name of this creek used for this special purpose is Evelequruq," Ayi said.

She then told them that while their papers were drying, she would ask the next person to share her recipe. Otherwise they would run out of time. And they could finish her picture-writing after Nupa had given her recipe.

"Ayi is gracious to let me win the drawing contest," Nupa commented humbly. "I know that I am not a better artist than she is." And smiling, she added, "But I will happily take home the Eskimo ice cream, and thank you to Panea."

Then Nupa began speaking.

"I am from Wales on the western tip of the peninsula. When I was little, our village just had an Inupiat name. But now, we are starting to use English names."

Nupa told them, "Start your drawing with Ipnatchiaq on the upper edge, and then draw your line going west." Nupa drew the bluff where the graveyard is located and kept going west, past a huge river called Goodhope River.

Then she drew another point, and said, "Start drawing your line south. There is a big village here, but it's not my village." Nupa was taking them on a long journey.

As she drew the line slowly, stopping and starting because the pencil would stop marking when it dried, she told them, "I am from the village where two shamans collided in midair. If they could fly like

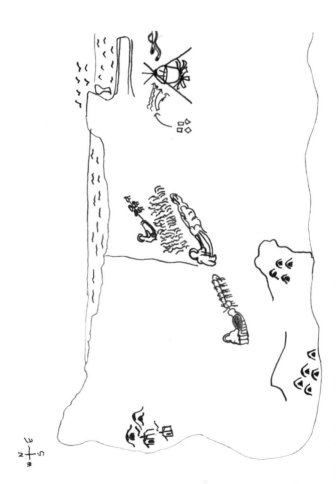

Nupa's Picture-Writing: *Reindeer Herding and Reindeer Soup* [DRAWING BY LORETTA OUTWATER COX]

that, then they both were very powerful shamans. They weren't from my village. One was from a village on an island and the other was from the north.

"Before my time," she continued, "my village was really two separate villages because of two powerful factions there. They were in constant war with each other for control of the other's part of the village. It was not a good situation. They hunted the bowhead whales that passed by every spring when they were two separate villages. They had a big competition to see which faction would catch the first whale. Openly, two sides of the village would not share the catch, but I knew that my mother and others shared secretly because they were related."

Nupa went on. "Then a reindeer herder named Mr. Lopp appeared and showed the people how to herd the reindeer that had been transported across from Siberia. My son, whose name is Karmana, became a reindeer herder. There was another reindeer herder there, so Karmana wanted to move his herd to Ipnatchiaq, and we came here.

"To draw a herd of reindeer," Nupa then said, "make an outline of the whole herd with different parts of the body on the outline. Draw motion by outstretching the front leg of some of the reindeer, and in the back of the herd draw the back leg outstretched on a few of them. Then draw the herd again about halfway to Ipnatchiaq. And draw at least three dog teams. That's how my son, with the help of relatives, moved the reindeer herd here.

"Now draw a big pot by our village," Nupa continued.

"And by the way," she said to her friends, "I want to thank everyone here for accepting me as one of you. It's not easy to leave all your family behind and to start all over again in a new place. When I first moved here, I was so homesick, mainly because my son, Karmana, was away with the reindeer herd most of the time. I think I started to be needed here when most everyone wanted to try making *mukluks* with reindeer skin. So I became very busy teaching other women. Therefore, I can thank my mother for teaching me how to sew *mukluks*. Now back to my recipe."

Nupa then said, "Draw chunks of reindeer meat right by the pot and draw water pouring into the pot. In the old days, we had no table salt and no rice, but draw a cup of rice and a little pile of table salt on a hand. This soup is so good," she concluded.

~~~~~~~~

Just then, Sikki heard Walter coming in the door. She told him to sit down and she would serve him some ptarmigan soup. Then he could go out and play.

All the women decided it was time to stand up and stretch because Ayi still had to finish speaking. Then Ne would give her recipe, and lastly Sikki would finish up for the day.

After a good break, they were seated again.

Ayi said, "I will now pass around a little cup of glue that I made with flour and water."

Everyone got busy pasting the gray river and the little gray creek on their pieces of brown paper for Ayi's story.

When that was done, Ayi passed around a little woven grass tray that was filled with slender, long, red leaves that had turned red in the fall. They were old sera leaves. The people picked sera leaves off the willows every spring and preserved them in seal oil. The leaves were their main vegetable through the long, dark winter.

The Storytellers pasted the red leaves on the gray river. The dry, red leaves looked like salmon swimming up the river.

Ayi then told them to take about ten of the little round leaves that were also on the tray. The round leaves came from *kavlak*, or bearberry bushes, which were bushes with big, black berries that no one ate because they didn't taste good.

"Now draw a round hole by Evelequruq Creek, and take some of this grass and put it in the bottom of the hole," she said, as she passed around the grass. "It's important to place the grass first, because it creates a pocket of air down in the hole. If the fish heads are aged with no air, they can turn poisonous and whoever eats them will surely die."

Ayi continued. "Paste the little round leaves on top of the grass. They are the fish heads. Then paste more grass over them. Then, on top of the grass, paste a circle of brown paper to signify that the fish heads are then covered with dirt. They will be ready to eat in a few days, and what a feast you will have!"

The Storytellers' eyes immediately went to Ne. She always sat to the right of Sikki.

"I knew we were going to share recipes today," she said. "I'm going to share stories of how my family and I gather greens."

Ne's Picture-Writing: *Sourdock and Immuruk Lake*
[DRAWING BY LORETTA OUTWATER COX]

Ne began by telling them, "Draw Ipnatchiaq and again make the river going to the south. And to the right of the river, draw a big lake."

Ne said that whenever her family walked to Immuruk Lake, they would make it a family outing because it was an all-day affair. "They started getting ready the day before," she explained, "making sure everyone had waterproof *mukluks* because the way would be wet in some places. And they made sure all their backpacks were ready. In the packs, they would bring a pot for boiling water, some matches, dried fish, boiled *ugruk* meat, hardtack crackers, and tin cups. And each person carried a little pot with a handle in case they found ripe berries to pick along the trail."

Then Ne said, "Now draw me, my husband with his gun, and two of our kids who liked to make that long walk. It took us about three hours or more to walk to Immuruk Lake.

"When we reached the lake," she told them, "first we made a fire and ate our lunch. Sometimes we would see wild animals there, so we made sure to take everything with us when we walked around the lake to pick sourdock. It was fun to pick sourdock at the big lake, because the leaves there grew so big it didn't take us long to gather a big supply.

"As we were picking the greens at the lake one day," Ne told them, "we heard a little voice. We looked at each other and asked whether anyone had said anything, and we all said 'no.' So we continued picking sourdock. But again, we heard the little voice."

Then Ne said, "I found where the little voice was coming from. Just as I was going to pick another handful of greens, the little voice said, 'Stop! You're picking where I live!'"

Ne said that she understood, and asked the little voice where they could pick the greens, because they had walked so far that day to pick them.

The little voice said, "Walk to the other side of the lake." And they did.

When everyone's backpack was full, they began the long walk back around the lake. Ne said that she forgot to try to speak again with the little voice because she couldn't believe what was happening. She said to the Storytellers, "Sometimes it is best not to question what is happening, but to go along with it. We did that, and nothing happened to us, and we got home safely."

Then Ne said, "Did I tell you to draw the sourdock by the lake? If I didn't, draw the long leaves and the tall stem with the seeds. And to draw the little voice, make some lines coming from behind the leaves."

Then she told them, "By the pot that you drew by the village, draw some chopped sourdock leaves. Draw water pouring into the pot and draw a stove under the pot. That is my recipe."

Then Ne added, "Oh, and yes, let's draw some blackberries in a bowl because that's how I put the cooked sourdock up for the winter, mixed with blackberries. Today, I brought you some sourdock with blackberries. Let's eat it right now!" Ne concluded.

Sikki went to get her wood bowls. She passed them to Ne, who served the cooked sourdock with blackberries. With that, they had a satisfying break.

When it was Sikki's turn to speak again, she told them how she and Walter had caught the ptarmigan she fixed for their soup today. "Last Saturday, when there was no school, I got my grandson ready to walk across the river with me to check my ptarmigan snares over in the willows. I noticed that Walter was going in a different direction. I asked him to come with me, but he said for me to go ahead and keep walking. When he caught up with me, I asked him why he went that way.

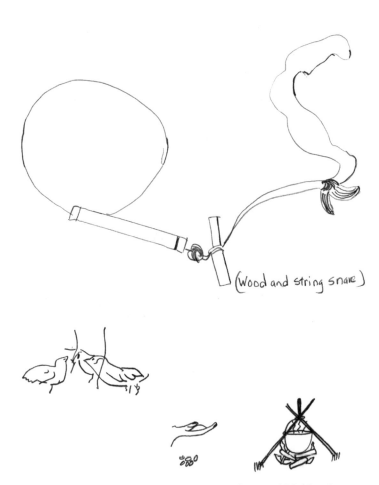

(Wood and string snare)

Sikki's Picture-Writing: *Snaring Ptarmigan and Making Soup*
[DRAWING BY LORETTA OUTWATER COX]

"Walter told me that when he plays outside, sometimes he would see Nupa walk across and go into some bushes. When he found her, he said she was praying and crying at the same time."

Sikki looked at Nupa and asked that she pray for her the next time when she went to say her prayers in her special spot in the willows.

"Lets draw a ptarmigan, just a ptarmigan," Sikki then said. "We all know that I snare them across the river in the willows. I think we're tired of drawing the Ipnatchiaq River. Near the ptarmigan, draw a few grains of rice and a pile of salt. That is my recipe for ptarmigan soup," Sikki said.

By the time they were through for the day with their picture-writing, it was almost dark. Sikki stood at the door as the Storytellers made their way out. Uto was the first to go through the door, and in a loud voice she said that their next meeting could be at her house.

Sikki followed her friends outside to see whether she could see or hear Walter playing. She felt thankful that she had someone to care for because all her own children were now adults and busy with their families elsewhere. When she saw him sliding down the riverbank with some friends, she waved and went back inside.

Once in her cozy house, she stoked the little stove and added more wood and coal. And before she rolled up everyone's papers, she looked at each drawing again.

"I wonder what the little voice was," she thought to herself. "That story reminds me of stories of the little people. Maybe we can share those stories someday."

Sikki felt so happy and fortunate that she had just spent a day with her friends, the Storytellers.

5

Relocating to Noorvik

It was a cold, snowy morning. Sikki put her parka on and went outside to bring in some ice chips for her water pot on the stove. She then went back out to get more firewood.

After taking off her parka, she sat down near her window. She began weaving her net with the balls of string that she had made from the flour bags. As she worked, once in a while she would look out the window. "Today I'm thankful to be sitting here in my own home," she told herself. And she began to remember a painful time in her life.

~~~~~~~

In 1913, May and Charles Replogle came to Ipnatchiaq. They replaced Martha Hunnicutt and Elizabeth Stratton, who had been the teachers and missionaries from 1911 to 1913.

Miss Hunnicutt, as she was called, believed that Christian holiness was a gift of grace made possible by Jesus Christ, and that this gift could be given instantaneously by faith. She also believed in and lived a plain Quaker lifestyle. Maxims in her life included "Remember the pleasant things in life," "Give others the sunshine, tell Jesus the rest," and "Don't let it be too hard to change thy mind." The Ipnatchiaq people remembered her as a scrupulous but loving person. Once she refused two bags of groceries bought by a Lomen Company employee because he was not Christian by her standard.

Sikki remembered that she and her friends had been more comfortable with the two female missionaries than the aggressive Mr. Replogle, who had arrived in the fall of 1913. People talked about how successful May and Charles Replogle had been in the Douglas, Alaska, Meeting of Friends in Southeast Alaska, in the years 1893 to 1902.

A story was told about Mr. Replogle: To ensure that the Indians in Douglas learned English, the students were told to get permission to speak in their Native tongue. Sometimes the students went into the wood-shed where they could talk "Indian talk." The Replogles prepared a solution of myrrh and capsicum to put on the tongues of those students who spoke the language that was forbidden by the government. Capsicum is pepper, and myrrh is a fragrant plant gum used in perfumes and incense.

At Ipnatchiaq, Charles Replogle then began writing letters in January 1914 to the Commissioner of Education, Mr. Claxton, in Washington, D.C. He wrote, "The Native can be colonized successfully and advantageously for himself and the Department." He wanted each colony, as he referred to a village, to have a graded school rather than the existing one-room schools. He wanted them to have a sawmill and facilities to manufacture stoves, soaps, sweets, and other items. All of these activities would result in business training. Alaska Natives were scattered in over 160 settlements, and he believed it would be too expensive to put schools in every place. He proposed that schools be put into 60 of the villages. From past experience at Hydaberg, Alaska, the schools would draw the people to the village where a school was set up.

Commissioner Claxton also argued in Washington, D.C., that the education of Native youths and adults in the United States and U.S. territories would therefore be more effective, because the federal Bureau of Indian Affairs (BIA) would place each school in the hands of a "man who has practical industrial training, a man of education fitted to become an industrial leader."

Before freezeup and just after their arrival, Charles and May Replogle had taken stock of conditions in the village. They decided that the local mining operations had made the Ipnatchiaq River too silty for fish, that the hunting was poor, that wood was too scarce for heat, and that the Native housing was crowded and unhealthy. After making these decisions for the Ipnatchiaq people, he began writing letters to Mr. Claxton. And at that time, Claxton appointed Charles Replogle as the industrial leader.

Four months later, in April 1914, the move began. Superintendent Shields reassigned Replogle, who proceeded to take the village schoolhouse apart and move it to a new location up the Kobuk River. Over the following two years, Replogle moved about two-thirds of the villagers of Ipnatchiaq along with all their property. According to Superintendent Shields, this was an important project: the government had channeled major resources to the new location, such as lumber and a reindeer herd. They brought 1,200 reindeer, and Bert Harvey was the chief herder. James E. Wells's parents named the new location Noorvik, meaning a place "to move to." Before the end of 1914, President Woodrow Wilson signed the order declaring Noorvik a BIA reservation for Alaska Natives.

The Bureau of Indian Affairs felt they were the protectors of Indians against every bad thing in Western culture. They believed Noorvik was a suitable place for the Natives because undesirable whites would be excluded. And the BIA teachers who were there had total control in their influence over the Native students.

People such as Superintendent Shields and Commissioner Claxton in Washington, D.C., believed in the BIA plan for the Ipnatchiaq Natives. That following their teachers out to the forest and tundra was best for the people. The third of the people who remained in Ipnatchiaq were older. After the move ended and there were no more disruptions, the small village of Ipnatchiaq on the seashore slowly began to develop again.

Sikki knew in her heart at the time that she should have remained in her village. Her older children were already gone and raising their own families. But her daughter Ruby, a single mother of two, was convinced she should go along with others who had young children. And Sikki didn't want to be separated from Ruby and her grandchildren. They were her family now and Ruby wanted her to come with them. So she did.

They packed up what they had, which wasn't much. They had their clothes, their bedding, and their kitchen dishes, pots, and utensils.

Along with some of her friends, she boarded the steamship *Cordova* and sailed for Qikitaġruq. Once out at sea, away from Ipnatchiaq, Sikki remembered vividly how beautiful her village looked. It was a good place, she remembered thinking.

It had taken Charles Replogle two years to disrupt everything and build up to this departure, so by the time Sikki and her little family got on the steamship, it was not a sad time. She had been very sad when they first heard of the plan, and especially when they watched them tear down the school. It had been especially sad when the Native men were no longer in charge of the village.

By the summer of 1915, Sikki had become used to the fact that their whole village had become uprooted.

The villagers who chose to remain in Ipnatchiaq realized they were "not imminently in harm's way." The Malemiut Inupiat who remained behind knew their ability to sustain themselves at Ipnatchiaq. Because of that, they felt free to choose their own future. By the time the move was complete, the river was becoming clear again. The salmon were coming back, and the *ugruk* hunt was as good as ever.

So, Sikki thought to herself, we moved to the place where they wanted us to follow the schoolhouse. In Noorvik the people were told to live by the clock, and a clock was put up in the middle of the village. It was a huge clock and you could not help but look at it whenever you walked through the village.

Noorvik was located in a beautiful area, on a river, with lots of spruce trees. There were plenty of fish in the river and they had abundant food to eat. Sikki remembered, I had enough wood to keep our place nice and warm. Since so much of our village had moved, mostly families with school-age children, I knew a lot of people there.

The people who were in charge told us that this place was good for us, she recalled. But as time went on, I began to feel that I wasn't in the right place for me. At first I kept my feelings to myself because I didn't want to be considered a troublemaker. We had always lived to help one another and not be a nuisance.

But pretty soon, I heard from others that they weren't happy either. So, I did not feel so bad when I sent word to my son, Ahkavluk, or Dick Mills, his English name, to come to Noorvik and bring me back home to Ipnatchiaq. He was living up the river at Kaniq. He soon came to Noorvik with his dog team. And that day, when we started traveling home by dogsled, was one of the happiest times in my life.

I wanted Ruby and her two children to return with me, but the children were going to go to school in Noorvik when they were old enough. And Ruby was getting married to Murphy Eterorock (whose name was later changed to Johnson by the Noorvik missionaries). Because I was assured that my children would be taken care of, I felt free to move back home. I was one of the first ones to move back, in 1916, just a year after leaving Ipnatchiaq. Some of the villagers moved back by dogsled that winter like I did, and some returned by boat the following summer.

Sikki sighed as she got up from weaving her net. She thought to herself, we should have known better than to let outsiders change our destiny in a time period of only four months. We have been here taking care of ourselves for thousands of years. We know how to deal with adversity, and if we didn't know how, we would have found a way. In the end, it should have been our choice to relocate Ipnatchiaq and not the decision of Superintendent Shields, Mr. Claxton, or President Woodrow Wilson. We must never forget that we are the ones who know best how to take care of our own. We should not be treated like little children incapable of deciding for ourselves, Sikki thought, scolding herself.

Now I am really back in my own little sod house in Ipnatchiaq, thought Sikki. That time was one of the hardest in my life. But now, I can hunt and fish with my Storytelling friends and relatives, and live out my life being happy back here in Ipnatchiaq.

When I first moved back to Ipnatchiaq, it wasn't easy, Sikki remembered. But with the help of the people like Uneyuq and his wife Ina, or Bessie Barr, who became like my family in the absence of my own, and also the Dimmick family, I was able to reestablish myself. When I moved back, there were more white people living in the village. They must really be making money from gold mining up the river, Sikki remembered thinking.

In the past, most of the miners left the village before freezeup. But many stayed over for the winter, to avoid a long ride on a ship out and back just to work for the summer. Sikki heard that a Japanese man with the last name of Okuda would be building a hotel and restaurant in the village to house miners who stayed over the winter.

By 1921, Sikki heard from travelers that her daughter Ruby was having a hard time up in Noorvik. So she sent word to her son Dick to travel up there to see if that was true. Sure enough, there was a hardship in her daughter Ruby's home. She still wanted to stay with Murphy Johnson, but she asked Sikki to bring her son Emuk back to Ipnatchiaq with her, saying that she and her older children would come home when they put a school in Ipnatchiaq again.

So, little Emuk lived with his grandmother in Ipnatchiaq, now called Deering, from the time he was two years old. By the time he turned six and was ready to go to school, there was a school-house in the village again, so Sikki began taking him to school.

6

Getting Ice

When Sikki awoke the next morning, it was dark. She found the matchbox and lit her kerosene lamp. Every time she lit that lamp, she was thankful for it. It was easier and quicker to light than her old clay seal oil lamp, especially in winter when the fire in the wood-stove had gone out by the time she woke up. Some cold mornings, she would be lucky to find embers still burning in the stove, which helped make a quick fire.

With the fire going, she heated water in her tin pot to make some coffee. Only in recent years had she started drinking coffee in the morning. She used to have tea. At Magid's store, they had Hills Brothers coffee and Gold Shield coffee. Her brand was Hills Brothers coffee, for no special reason.

Sikki noticed she was running out of water, so she'd need to take a trip upriver to get ice for her drinking and cooking water. She told herself that after her grandson had gone to school that day, she would make that trip.

Some days she fretted whether to wake Walter up for school. He always looked so comfortable sleeping in his soft reindeer sleeping bag. But she knew it was important for Walter to go to school to learn to read and write, now that their lives seemed to be going in that direction. Sikki couldn't read the words on her coffee can, but she knew what they sounded like because the storekeeper would ask whether she wanted Hills Brothers coffee. And she knew it said "flour" on the bags that she unraveled for her net, but she didn't know the sounds of the individual letters. So that's why it was important for her to wake up Walter.

"Wake up, Walter," she gently said. Sikki recalled that his mother had been like Walter when she was small—hard to wake up.

"Wake up, Walter," Sikki repeated, but this time with a gentle nudge to his arm. "Here's some warm milk, Walter," she said in Inupiaq.

He sat up sleepily and took the warm milk.

When Walter got up, Sikki had some warm water for him in the wooden basin they used for washing. Another item that made their lives easier was the dishtowel they used for washing their hands and faces. They had one dishtowel for the dishes and one for them.

Before they left the house for school, Sikki put two more pieces of wood in the stove so the fire wouldn't go out while she was gone. As they walked toward the schoolhouse, they were glad it wasn't windy. When the wind blew in their coastal village, it was sometimes hard to walk, especially when it was a west wind or a north wind. You'd have to walk leaning into the wind to keep your balance. It was a good distance to the school in the middle of the village.

As they walked, other children joined them with a friendly "hi." The children now greeted each other in English. Since there was no wind, Sikki could hear the squeak and crunch of their *mukluks* as they stepped on the frozen snowy ground. And once in a while, someone's dog would howl and then all the other dogs in the village howled.

They finally reached the school, and Sikki told Walter she would be walking up the river to get ice after she walked back home. Then she stood outside as he went in the school with the other children.

As she walked home, she thought of the picture-writing that the Natives do when they are studying the Bible. Sikki thought about what she had learned when they were across the bay and up the river at Noorvik, when they were relocated to the reservation. Sikki had kept a piece of paper with one of the pictures on it. She thought it was so interesting that she could look at a piece of paper and know what the picture-writing meant.

Sikki could remember the time before the missionaries came. They said that they brought the Word of God, including the Ten Commandments. The first commandment was to honor your father and your mother. Sikki thought about how the missionaries had not brought that idea to the people, because she and all her Storyteller friends already honored their fathers and their mothers. That was the highest form of respect in their culture, and it would be their turn in the future to be respected.

Their parents were like them, the Storytellers. In all their times together, when one of them remembered something about her parents, it usually concerned what the parents had taught them and how they had listened when they were told to do something. When they were children, there were no schools. The children observed what their parents did and simply learned that way.

Everyone was very busy in the old days. The young boys and young men learned to hunt and to make hunting gear in the *qasgi*, where there was a distinct hierarchy from the elder to the young boy. The elders taught the young boys to feel special because they would someday be the providers. For instance, when duck soup was served as the meal at home, the young boy would have the choice part—the duck head and the tasty brain. The early people did not have any spices to flavor their food, but they knew what parts of the animal tasted delicious.

The young girls helped with raising the children and became assistants to their parents. They learned early how to take good care of their younger brothers and sisters. And the younger children knew that they had to listen to the older sister who was taking care of them. All of this organization came from their parents, who in turn learned it from their parents. Sikki recalled that one of the Storytellers remarked that respect and honor came naturally for these young children because they were with their parents all day long and all night long. There was no way to learn disrespectful ways when someone was watching them and guiding them at all times.

When Sikki reached her sod house, she went in to put more wood in the stove. Then outside, she secured a container on her little homemade sled she used for getting ice. The container, a large woven bag, was made of beach grass.

Walking down the riverbank, she was careful not to slip and fall. There was still no wind, so she could hear her *mukluks* breaking the crust on the snow that had formed after the last storm. She knew it would take her a while to walk the half mile upriver to the spot where she got clean river ice. She often looked back toward the village just for the view. During the dark times when there was hardly any hunting going on, people slept later in the morning. Occasionally she'd meet someone else who was also going to fetch ice, but today she could see there was no one else heading that way.

That was okay with her. She was still thinking about the Ten Commandments the missionaries had told them about. Right now there was no missionary in Ipnatchiaq.

One commandment was that no one should kill another person. Her people did, on occasion, kill *itkiliqs,* or Indians, that came from inland, and the *itkiliqs* killed some of her people, it was known. Sikki knew that they had fought over hunting grounds for generations. She also knew that some of the young men in her village went out scouting to see whether *itkiliqs* were coming to their village.

It was winter and very cold now, and Sikki was thankful for that. As she walked slowly upriver, her mind wanted to finish her thoughts about the commandment, "Thou shalt not kill." In the story that her husband, Utli, had told about the giants, it was clear that the wives rebelled against the giant's demand that they kill their boy babies, and that they had conspired to kill him because he was a bad person. So you knew that you had to be a good member of your village and not cause grief or unnecessary harm, or someone might kill you. This was never discussed, but each member understood that it was better to be a contributing citizen. This lesson was learned as you were growing up, first by observing and then by becoming the teacher of others born into their society.

Another commandment said, "Thou shalt not commit adultery." This was a foreign concept just one generation ago, when her mother was young. In those days, the young men could have as many wives as they could provide for. And wives lived together like the wives in Utli's story of the giants. It was a lifestyle for survival.

According to the missionaries, having more than one wife at a time was a sin. She knew that her daughter's friend Tosalviq's father had another wife, but in another village. A lot of times it happened that way. When a hunter regularly traveled far for game, he would have another wife at that location. In the instance of Tosalviq, or Lily Egaq, (daughter of Qutla and Egaq), after going to school and studying the Bible with the white missionaries in a village south of the Seward Peninsula, she was ashamed that her father had another wife. The way she handled the situation was to just not talk about it openly. The family kept the issue to themselves. And when the people saw relatives from a father having two wives, they treated each other with dignity and respect.

When Sikki reached the place in the river where the people got clean ice for drinking water, she got the *touq* out of her sled, which was a big stick with a sharp metal point that her husband had made. She also used this tool to make holes in the river ice for tomcod fishing. This implement was as important to her as her *ulu*, or curved knife, which she used every day. As she chipped at the ice, she could see a trace of sunlight in the east. On these dark days, it was good to get even a glimpse of a sunrise.

As the ice chips grew into a pile, she used her big wooden ladle to scoop them into her grass bag. It usually took ten piles of ice chips to fill up the grass bag. And now that she was getting older, she rested occasionally while she did her work. Sikki knew that one of the young men would get her ice for her, but she had enjoyed being independent her whole life and wanted to do things for herself. She was happy that she could still do this work. And besides, she loved being outdoors.

As she walked back toward the village, she slowly pulled the bag of ice chips on her little sled. It wasn't hard work, and the system worked well.

Let me see, she began recalling again. One of the commandments was that one should not tell lies about her neighbor. There was nothing new there. In their society, lives were intertwined in order to help one another survive. There wasn't room for lies about one's neighbor. As she thought of all her Storyteller friends, she could think of no one who would intentionally hurt others by telling lies about them.

Sikki could see the outline of the village against the white ocean and the dark sky, with the hint of glowing light from the east. It wouldn't be daylight for another two or three hours. She was slowly making progress toward home.

She thought about the commandment, "Thou shalt not steal." When she was little, she remembered her mother, Ekiyuq, talking with her about this. One fall, while they gathered food for the winter, they were out looking for a storehouse of the field mice. When they found one, they knew it would be full of *musu*, or wild potatoes, all bite-size and sweet. The mice knew when the *musu* had the best taste, and dug them up to store them for the winter. Her mother wouldn't take the whole store of wild potatoes from the mice, but left some, and even added some dried meat or fish in place of the potatoes she took.

Ekiyuq told Sikki, "It would be stealing if we took all the potatoes in the storehouse. Hunters and travelers, who go long distances and stop to rest in the shelters that everyone shares, are often treated with some food left behind that doesn't spoil quickly. It was their duty to then replace what they had eaten with some other food, so that the next traveler would have something to eat." Everyone tried to help one another survive, and so stealing just wasn't part of their behavior.

Back home, Sikki went inside to get her metal bucket with the wooden ladle hanging from it. She left the ladle and took the bucket outside to fill it with ice chips. The place where she kept her ice chips sack was on the side of her house where she could watch it from the window. Then, in case there was a dog loose, she could see it and chase it away. The place where she chopped her wood was on the other side of the house, so wood chips wouldn't fly into her ice bag or break her window. And she kept her sack of coal there also. She tried not to burn coal quickly so that the sack would last through the colder days of the year.

With the ice-gathering chore done, Sikki came inside and took off all her cold-weather gear. In her little home, there was a place for her to hang up their parkas, and their *mukluks* were placed on the floor below the parkas.

Sikki was eager to find that piece of paper she had remembered, which had the Bible verse, John 3:16, in picture-writing. She wished she knew more about it. When she found the piece of paper among her treasures, she looked at it carefully.

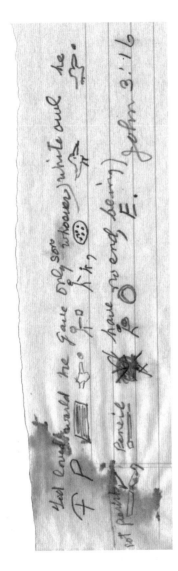

Picture-Writing by Sikki's grandson Walter and his wife, Ruth Outwater, done in 1984, Nome, Alaska (some water damage): *The Bible, John 3:16.* "And God so loved the world, he gave his only begotten son, that whosoever believeth in him shall not perish but will have life everlasting." [DRAWING COURTESY OF RUTH OUTWATER]

First there was a symbol that resembled a cross with an arc over it. The Storytellers had learned that the great God of the missionaries had sent his son to Earth, and that the son had been nailed to a cross and had died. He was nailed to the cross so that everyone, even those who came from the village, could go to Heaven. The missionaries preached about Heaven, explaining that it was a good place to go when you die.

Sikki and her people, for centuries, had talked about the Great Man in the Sky, who was in charge of everything. They believed that, because of the Great Man in the Sky, they had a reverence for all things on Earth. So when the missionaries brought this belief, it wasn't hard for Sikki's people to come to accept the missionaries' God. The arc over the cross was drawn to depict this great God, and his son was depicted by the cross.

Sikki looked at the next symbol in the drawing, and she had a hard time remembering what it signified. She remembered that the Native person who was a helper to the missionary tried to explain it to them. The symbol stood for something in the white man's culture that they had never heard of before. There was a vertical straight line. At the top of the line, a curved line went in a half circle and reconnected to the straight line about halfway down.

"What did they call it?" Sikki asked herself. "I'll ask my grandson when he comes home from school whether he can remember what this symbol stands for."

The next picture was a parallelogram with lines from left to right. This symbol stood for a piece of ground, *nuna* in the Inupiaq language. At that time, no one knew the world was round. They just understood that the world was the piece of dirt under their feet. The drawing said, this "God so loved the world."

"Oh—loved," Sikki repeated to herself. In Inupiaq, "love" is pronounced *pitka*. So that was the second symbol—a "P." She would still ask Walter if he studied that symbol in school. It was an English language letter. "So this God loves everyone, even all the people in my village," she said.

The Inupiaq word *elan* means "pointing." Sikki looked at the pointing finger in the picture-writing. It was connected to the rest of the folded fingers and part of an arm. The finger was pointed at a single dot. *Elan* also meant "he" in the English language, because he is pointing. In this case, "He" was the missionary's God.

The next drawing was a stick figure of a person standing sideways, with a head, a vertical line for his neck and back, and then one leg back. The other leg was extended in front. The arms together held a box in front of him. This symbol meant "gave."

Then there were two stick figures of a man and his small son. They are both standing sideways, and the man's arm slanted down toward the son. There was a comma after the little son. Above the pair were the words "only son." This part of the message meant, "He gave his only son."

"*Kisupiaq*, or "everybody," the next symbol, was a round circle with six dots in it. It stood for and really means, "It is given to everybody." In English, it means "whoever." Then *ukpiksiroaq*, which meant "believeth."

The next drawing was an owl. "White owl" was written above the owl drawing; *ukpik* in Inupiaq means "owl."

After that, the symbol for "he" was repeated, the finger pointing at a dot. Above the hand, it said "he." Together it stood for "whosoever believeth in Him."

Piyuqquominaachuq, which came next, in Inupiaq means "not perish." Then there was a little boat and a check by the little boat. Beside that was a drawing of the little boat sinking in the water, with the check mark sinking also. Above the drawings were the words, "not perish." Next there was a picture of a pencil. In Inupiaq, *ugloin* means "pencil," which is equivalent to the English word "but." It is pronounced *uh-glan.*

Then another stick figure was drawn standing sideways holding something round. "Have" was written above that figure. The next symbol was a set of two circles that were intertwined with no beginning and no end, meaning "no end," which is written above. Everlasting life was depicted by the picture-writing, concluding with a capital letter "E" and a period, which in Inupiaq is said *esuetchomic,* and above that was written "end." At the end, there was a closed parenthesis sign, meaning "life" or "being." This part of the message means, "not perish but have no end to life."

The picture-writing records a passage in the Bible from the book of John, chapter 3, verse 16, which in English is usually written: "For God so loved the world, he gave his only begotten son, that whosoever believeth in him shall not perish but will have life everlasting."

When Sikki finished reading and thinking about the old picture-writing, she realized she had lost track of time. And she was also hungry. But it was almost time for Walter to come home because the day was dark again. She decided to just make herself some fresh tea. She would have ptarmigan soup with her grandson later. Her fire was burning just right. It wasn't making her little place overly warm.

I'll just lie down and wait for Walter, she thought to herself. It wasn't long before Sikki was asleep, dreaming of a time when she and Utli and her three young children were together.

Coming into the sod house, Utli said to his wife, Sikki, "We can go to Pingue today. There is a little wind from the west."

As he spoke these words, Sikki smiled. They had planned this trip for a week. It was late summer, and the village people usually made this journey at this time of the year. She knew others would travel today also. She was looking forward to it.

So Sikki got herself ready first, letting the children sleep longer. The youngest child loved to sleep, and often they just let her sleep. That's how the youngest was treated in their culture, and typically the baby ended up being spoiled by all members of the family.

Since they had been packing their supplies for a week, all they had to do was get dressed and go down to their skin boat, or *umiaq*. Sikki had the dried caribou and hardtack packed and ready for breakfast, so they could eat after they were on their way. The children were happy when they learned where they were going that day. They always had fun on this yearly trip. A lot of other children would be there.

After helping with blackberry picking every day, the children liked to play *mana-mana* on the wide beach. In this game, there are two sides. On each side, a team is in the middle of a circle. Each person tries to run around the other team's circle for a point. If that person is tagged by the other team, he is sent "to jail" in a circle on the side. If his teammates make it to jail, he or she can go back to the home circle and run to make a point again. The children loved to play this game, and they couldn't wait to get to Pingue.

The time it took to get to this place depended on how strong the west wind was blowing. On this day it wasn't very strong, so they hoped it would become a little stronger, but not too strong or the waves would be too big. As they traveled out of the Ipnatchiaq River and into the ocean, Utli used a long pole as a rudder to turn the *umiaq* so it faced east. Then he told Sikki and their son to pull the sail up. When the sail was up and filled with wind, and they were sailing smoothly, Sikki fed her family breakfast.

They would probably camp at Pingue for about a week, depending on the weather. Sometimes, in late summer, it would rain there for many days in a row. It was possible to pick blackberries in the rain; it was just harder to clean them, because dirt, wet grass, and twigs would stick to the delicate, wet fruit. But everyone would be warm and dry. They had raingear made from beluga intestines and *mukluks* made of waterproof red sealskin.

As they were traveling, sure enough they saw three other *umiaqs* with their sails up. It was a happy day. Waves lapped at the bow of the boat as they moved forward, and even that noise sounded happy. On the shore, everyone watched for any animals that might be walking along. They knew they would probably see at least two or three red fox, and they needed to watch for seals in the water. If any seals were close enough for the father or the son to throw a harpoon, they would have fresh seal meat for dinner. Or if someone in the other three *umiaqs* got a seal, they would all share the fresh meat. The women would help cut up the seal after the hunter had given it a ladle of water to help it on its journey to the spirit world of the seal.

When they first got there, there was always driftwood to collect. The children gathered all the wood for their fires while they stayed there.

The men cut the roots off the big spruce trees that had drifted there. The roots would then be taken back to the village and the men brought them to the *qasgi*, where they carved them into all types of pots, dishes, or ladles, depending on the shape of the roots.

At the camp, they had a big metal pot they were all thankful for that they used to cook their meals. Two or three of the men would make a tripod out of straight poles, and then they hung the pot from it on a loop. They all anticipated how good the fresh, cooked meat and blubber would taste. It was too late in the season to pick greens, so each of the women would have brought some from her supply at home.

As they approached a river, Sikki briefly remembered her childhood, because it was there at that bluff where she spent a lot of time with her cousin Qutla from another village. They used to go there to make clay pots. Her cousin's mother was famous for her pots in this region.

But as soon as they sailed past the spot, she didn't think of Qutla anymore. Sikki wanted to enjoy this day with her family. The children were enjoying the trip even though they had to sit still. They were watching the other *umiaqs* now, wondering whether they would catch up to them.

When the children were small, the village was all Inupiat people. So their lives were predictable. The village followed traditional activities and traded with other villages. There were still trade fairs in the village up north. Sikki used to enjoy going there with her mother and her mother's family. That was where her mother and Utli's parents arranged their marriage. The people were accustomed to traveling a lot, and so Sikki was enjoying this day.

As she and Utli were smiling at each other, a noise awoke her. Her grandson Walter was home from school. As she sat up, it took her a moment to realize she had been dreaming. "I must've gotten tired from walking up the river and pulling back that bag of ice back home," she thought.

"Hi grandma," Walter said, smiling.

Sikki asked him, "How was school today?"

"It was okay," he said. "I was thinking about you getting ice. Can we get ice when I'm not in school the next time?" he asked.

She smiled at him and nodded her head, yes. "Before you go back out to play," she said, "let's eat. I've been waiting for you to come home and I'm hungry."

While Sikki and Walter were eating, she told him about her dream. It was as though her husband, Utli, had come back for a visit, she realized. Everything seemed so real, from the blue water of the sea to the sound of the water lapping against the boat.

7

Muga

As Sikki lived every day, she did her chores in the same routine. After leaving her grandson Walter at the schoolhouse and walking east back to her house, she could feel the wind on her face. Not a day went by that she did not feel grateful to be back in her own village by the sea. Looking out at the ocean this morning, she could see two dog teams traveling east, probably going to Kugruq, the next river over, to ice fish for tomcod. If they were her friends' husbands, she thought, the tomcod would be shared with her.

When she reached her home, first she stoked the woodstove. Then she brought in more wood from the woodpile. Next she brought in some ice chips to melt in the big pot that remained on the stove so she always had water available.

Sitting down by the window, she picked up one of her flour sacks and searched for the beginning of the fabric so she could unravel the bag and make a ball of string. This morning, her thoughts went back to her mother, Ekiyuq, who related a story that impressed on her the importance of family and friends. It was about the father her mother never knew, the man who was Sikki's grandfather.

In the old days, there was a young couple. His name was Ahgavluq and her name was Kitiruaq. They had a daughter who was not yet a teenager. A niece also lived with them whose name was Ikpiqkosuq. She was about fourteen or fifteen years old.

Autumn came. There was a big whaling ship going by. As the ship went along at the other side of a bluff, it became stranded. It was a huge ship with sails.

They discovered it was useless to try to pull the ship off the beach. The other sailors tried to convince the captain to go back with them on one of their ships, but he would not budge. His sailors went on another ship, but he stayed behind.

As winter came and the ocean froze, the Native people visited the man. They tried to communicate with him. They learned that his name was Mr. Moore. They couldn't pronounce that, so to them he became "Muga."

The teenage girl, Ikpiqkosuq, and her younger cousin began visiting Muga on the ship. He treated them with sweets, maybe candy, and they became friends. Muga was especially fond of the teenage girl. As winter progressed, the younger girl noticed that during each of their visits, Muga took Ikpiqkosuq to another cabin on the ship for a while.

In the spring, after breakup, the ice went out. The other whaling ships returned, and their friend Muga left. The Natives thought that he had come from Siberia, but they found out he was from England. He had red hair and his language was English.

After he left, the village found out that Ikpiqkosuq was carrying Muga's baby. A baby girl was born, and she was named Ekiyuq.

Sikki had always known this story. Her mother, Ekiyuq, made sure Sikki knew about her grandmother,

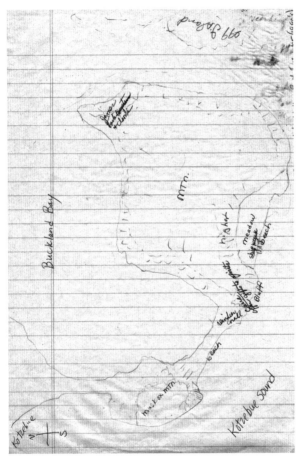

Hand-drawn map by Sikki's grandson Walter and his wife, Ruth Outwater, 1990s: *Captain Moore's ship, the HMS Plover, is beached at Chamisso Island in Kotzebue Sound, 1849–52, around the time of the Franklin Expedition.* [DRAWING COURTESY OF RUTH OUTWATER]

Ikpiqkosuq, her other ancestors, and all her other relatives. Sometimes Sikki heard her parents and her cousin's parents talking about it while they camped together at the place where they made clay pots, east of Ipnatchiaq at the next river over.

In those years, starting about 1848, as many as 50 whaling ships went by, and by 1852 the people saw as many as 200 whaling ships in their waters. The Natives were very curious about these ships. Sikki's family thought that Captain Moore's ship was a whaling ship, but it was really a depot ship called the HMS *Plover*. It was from England on a seven-year voyage to the Bering Strait and the western Arctic. There were many ships sent to look for the ships of the Franklin Northwest Expedition (1845–48) that had disappeared. The names of the lost ships were the HMS *Erebu* and the HMS *Terror*. They were last seen by a British whaler north of Baffin Bay, a far-away place. So the *Plover* was one of the ships helping in the search for the Franklin Expedition, and asking the Natives if they had heard anything about those two ships.

The young couple in the story, Ahgavluq and Kitiruaq, were Qutla's great-great-grandparents. Their people were nomads who traveled here and there, depending on what game, fish, or foods they were seeking.

The couple had offered Muga their help because that's how the people were. No doubt there was curiosity about this person who would not leave his ship and lived on it by himself all winter. Later in life, Sikki found out that contrary to the "shipwreck" story, Muga, or Commander Thomas Edward Laws Moore, along with Captain Henry Kellett, had decided that the *Plover* would winter on the east side of Chovis Peninsula.

After Muga had gone with Kellett aboard the HMS *Owen* and surveyed the Buckland River, they came back to the *Plover* and built a supply house on shore, where they stored most of their provisions. The *Plover*'s mast was also taken down for the winter. The ship was then much lighter, so they were able to move her into twelve feet of water, closer to the shore.

Toward the middle of June 1852, Muga watched in horror as breakup ice pushed the ship to shore again, nearly crushing her. Later that summer, a ship called the *Amphitrite* skippered by Rochfort Maguire sailed in and relieved Commander Moore, who departed the North Country in September.

Sikki wondered whether Qutla's ancestors Ahgavluq and Kitiruaq had met Muga when he was surveying up the Buckland River that summer and had made arrangements to visit him, rather than meeting him for the first time where the *Plover* was settled in to spend the winter. Sikki had heard how friendly the Buckland people were, and that made more sense to Sikki. They must have made a shelter close by, and that's how they got to know this man the Natives called Muga.

Sikki began thinking about her grandmother, Ikpi, or Ikpiqkosuq, and how she came to be with this man, Muga. She thought to herself, Ikpi's parents were probably no longer alive. If they were, they would have already arranged her marriage to some young Native man.

In the new way, Sikki's children were with mates they had chosen themselves, Sikki thought. For a quick moment, she blamed herself for not working out arranged marriages for her children. Maybe if Utli had lived longer, things would have turned out differently for my children, she said to herself.

Oh well, she concluded, with a sigh.

~~~~~~~

I am almost to the end of the flour sack I have been unwinding, Sikki thought. That's for the best, she decided.

As she reflected on thoughts about her roots, she chuckled as she recalled a comment Ayi had made about Walter.

"I thought Walter was supposed to be part *naluagmiu*, or white," Ayi would tease. She said that to Sikki in the springtime after Walter had been playing out all day and his face was darker than the faces of the rest of the children.

8

Qutla's Visit

"*Iglaak*!" Sikki heard someone outside hollering.

Again she heard "*Iglaak*!" That meant someone from another village was traveling toward Ipnatchiaq.

Sikki laid down the net she was working on, put on her parka, and quickly went outdoors. She could see a dog team coming around the bend of the river at the point. Soon she saw that her cousin Qutla was sitting in the sled, and that Qutla's husband, Egaq, was standing at the back of the sled.

As she watched them travel closer, she waved at her cousin, who was already waving to her. Still coming closer, they smiled at each other, and Sikki smiled at

Egaq too. Sikki felt grateful to him for bringing Qutla for a visit.

When the dog team stopped at her house, all three of them started talking at once. They were all so happy, and the dogs seem to sense the happiness too. They unharnessed the dogs and tied each one to a stake in the yard. Then they continued visiting, outside.

Qutla told Sikki, "We are going up north to visit Tusalviq and Savokenaq, or Lily and John Savok, who were in Qikiqtaġruk for a while. Egaq wanted to check on his daughter's family to see how they are doing. I thought we might keep going west to see you, since we had to make a stop at Elephant Point to get some white beluga whale *muktuk* from our storage place. The Kaniq people store the springtime catch in that location because it is a good spot for storing food. After leaving Kaniq, our village, we camped one night at Elephant Point."

"Two other dog teams traveled down the river from Kaniq to get some *muktuk* too," Egaq said. "But they started back up the river after they had dug out their food from the snow. I think they wanted to go as far as Elephant Point to help me dig in our storage place. The younger people have begun helping me a lot, and this dogsled trip may be my last. It isn't easy running the dog team nowadays," Egaq admitted.

Qutla said to Sikki, "Here's some *muktuk* for you and some dried smelt."

Sikki held out her hands, and said, "*Quyana*," with a grateful look on her face. "Let's go inside now," she said. And they kept talking as they entered the little sod house.

"How long will you be staying here?" Sikki asked.

"We could stay two or three nights," Qutla answered.

Egaq said, "I'll ask around to see whether anyone is traveling to Qikiqtaġruk. Hopefully we won't have to travel alone. It was okay coming from Elephant Point by ourselves because it's not far. But I don't want to go a long distance alone, in case something might happen."

"How are the Kaniq people and what are they doing?" Sikki asked, full of questions.

"Wait," she interrupted herself. "Let me make some coffee while you two take off some of your layers of clothing. You can hang them over here on the wall.

"*Hee, hee, hee ha*!" said Sikki, laughing and pointing to the wall. "You can see I have some nails for hanging clothes," she explained. "I have been learning a lot from my neighbor, the old white miner who lives here year-round. He likes to pick the mushrooms that grow on my roof, and he gave me some of his nails. His name is Frank Henry."

Soon they were seated on caribou skins on the floor. Sikki had at least six nice skins for the Storytellers. Sikki poured them all some coffee.

Egaq answered, "The Kaniq people are fine. There has been no sickness this winter. And everyone has food. That is another reason for this trip to Qikiqtaġruk, to trade some white *muktuk* and smelt for dried *ugruk* meat in seal oil. If there is someone here in the village who would like to trade with us, that would be even better, because then we wouldn't have to travel up north."

After they had their coffee, Sikki said, "Do you want to rest? Go ahead and lie down on my bed here on the floor. I will cook some tomcod while you rest."

As Sikki was busy cooking, Walter came home from school. He was surprised to see their visitors and happy too because his grandmother was happy.

"Today, you may bring in some wood," Sikki said to Walter. "We'll have dinner when Qutla and Egaq wake up from their nap. Stay home instead of playing outside, so you can listen and learn from Egaq."

While Sikki was cooking, Walter sat outdoors, and when his friends called him, he told them he couldn't play today. He observed the dogs, curled up and sleeping. He didn't go near them because he was afraid of them. Sled dogs can be aggressive to strangers. But he told himself that when he grew up, he would own a dog team. Maybe, he thought, Egaq will let me help feed the dogs this evening.

Sikki sat down, and as she was cutting up the *muktuk*, she still couldn't believe that her friends were taking a nap in her house. She was thankful for the food they had brought from Kaniq.

Soon the water started boiling, so she put whole tomcods in the water with some salt from Magid's store. Then she placed the *muktuk* on a wooden platter that Utli had carved. And she set everything on a low wooden platform that was their table.

When she saw her friends beginning to wake up, she told them, "When you are ready to eat, the food is all set."

After they were seated at the table, Sikki called Walter in. He looked at the people who were his grandmother's friends and relatives and therefore related to him too. Sikki had taught Walter well, so he acknowledged them politely. After a "hi" as a greeting, Walter remained quiet and attentive. Sikki was raising him to be quiet around older people, and he was learning well.

Egaq spoke to Walter first. "Young man, I have a story for you," he said.

Qutla looked at Walter and said, "What a nice looking boy my cousin Sikki is raising."

While they ate, Egaq began to tell Walter a story of the old way of hunting beluga whales at Elephant Point.

My father had a *kayaq*. Once they camped in the spring at Shisolik, which was by the bay. Boats can go into this deep river. People always camp where they can have fresh water. Kaniq people like big families so they will have successful hunts together. Shisolik was a good location to watch for beluga, or the white whale.

The day finally came when the beluga whales started coming into the bay after the ice went out. They came in with the tide and everyone was happy. In those days, the people's boats were not made of lumber. They had big skin-covered *umiaqs* and *kayaqs*.

The people would build the frame of a big boat or of a *kayaq*. We worked on them in a *qasgi*, where only men and boys were allowed. I wish I could take you there, Walter. The boat frame was made out of birch wood from way up the river from Kaniq. We made the frame by hand and tied everything together with strips of seal hide. We didn't use nails like your grandma has on the walls. We covered the *umiaq* frame with walrus skin, which we had traded for from people who live by the seacoast.

Eventually, when the skin boat covering became old and worn, we took it off and used it for flooring in our houses. There were many uses for an old *umiaq* cover. We used things over and over again. No part of any animal was ever wasted.

We covered the *kayaq* frame with the skin of a young *ugruk*, or bearded seal, using the same stitch as for the *umiaq*. For sewing, sinew was made from caribou and beluga tendons. There are four areas in the beluga's back where there are large pieces of meat and huge tendons. The tendons were scraped clean of meat and dried. The women separated the tendons and prepared it to make sinew. The pieces of sinew were braided, which makes a very strong thread. It was used to sew items such as waterproof *mukluks*, *kayaqs*, and *umiaqs*.

A *kayaq* is agile and very tough. It's also so light that it can be easily hauled up on land or on the ice by just one hunter. And if the hunter has his spray skirt attached to the hole where he sits, the *kayaq* is unsinkable even if he rolls over.

Before a hunter could take his *kayaq* out to sea, he had to come up with his own markings, in case something happened to him at sea. We made sure his markings were put on all his hunting gear to protect him from dangerous sea spirits. That's what we believed. But now our beliefs are changing because people are learning the missionary way, like what Qutla preaches.

Also in the old days, while we were hunting the beluga, we were not allowed to chop wood, dig in the earth, sew, tan skins, and many other things, for fear the spirits that controlled the movement of the beluga would take offense and not permit the whales to return the next season.

When all the hunters were ready, they told the children and their wives not to make any noise because the belugas would pass our camping place. The *kayaqs* and the hunters would all be by the water. One hunter would lead, and five or six others followed one at a time. Just like rounding up reindeer, they drove the belugas into shallow water.

Then they used a spear connected to a long rawhide rope to make the kill. At the end of the rope, an *ugruk* bladder bag was attached so the whale wouldn't sink. The hunters each chose a whale to go after. They could tell how big each whale was by the size of its dorsal fin. And everyone helped each other so that each hunter would catch a beluga.

Some years the whales were scarce. So when a person brought the first catch home, it belonged to everyone in the village. Every part of the beluga whale was used. Finally, we made a big bag out of the whale's stomach, and the meat was stored in it.

When the whaling was completed, the people collected the bones and burned them to honor the whale. Those who could afford to, burned the clothes they wore while whaling. Those who were poor cut off a small piece of a garment, to pay tribute to the beluga.

By the time Egaq was through with his story, they had finished eating the boiled tomcod and the white *muktuk*. Sikki had been eating dried smelt from the Kaniq people, because that was one of her favorite foods.

Egaq said, "I hope you will come to Elephant Point when you become a whale hunter, Walter."

9

Getting Wood

One day, Sikki noticed that it was time for her to collect more firewood. She would go to the spot where they gathered driftwood, by the sea.

As she pulled her little sled along the shore toward Kippalu, the bluff near the big rock that's bigger at the top than at the bottom, she thought about the story of the three giants. People said that their dwelling was at the west end of the village. As she continued to walk on the frozen seashore, she hoped she wouldn't see the three giants' father as an *aleuqtuk,* or ghost.

Don't be silly, Sikki told herself. There won't be an *aleuqtuk,* because the father was not mean like his three sons. Sikki believed *aleuqtuks* could walk through rock and wood. That was what the people said when they told scary stories.

Once in a while, a cold wind would reach Sikki's face through her wolverine and wolf fur ruff. She thought the wind was calling her name, "*Sikki*," as she believed it did once in a while. She loved the wind. She felt like it had kept her company after Utli died.

This time, it was not the wind calling her name, but her friend Uto. She looked back, and her friend hollered, "Wait, Sikki! I want to get some wood with you!

"I looked out my glass window," Uto said, when she got closer, "and I saw you walking with your sled. So I put on my parka and mitts so fast, I think my husband thought something was happening!"

They laughed together, and Sikki said, "For once, I'm glad it wasn't the wind calling my name."

As they walked, Sikki said to Uto, "I am happy to have company today. I was thinking about how doing my chores is getting a little harder for me now. And that was making me think about death."

Sikki continued, "I remember hearing old people up north talk about *Aniragvik*. They say that's where people go when they die. *Aniragvik* means 'a place where people come from.' So if it means 'a place where people come out from,'" she said, "my husband, must have gone back where he came from."

Uto knew she shouldn't interrupt Sikki when she was feeling this way, so she pulled her sled and walked with her head bowed against the wind.

"See that pile of driftwood over there?" Sikki asked Uto.

Uto looked where Sikki pointed. They both knew what it was. It was where a family put its loved one when that person died. The teepeelike structure of driftwood was rotting away and falling to the ground in soft chunks.

"I've seen piles of driftwood wherever I've been," Sikki said. "They are on the other side of the bluff, across the bay, and around Kugruq and Pingue. Probably anywhere our people hunt for food."

Sikki then said, "Do you want to hear a story told to my cousin Qutla and me by her mother, Paneluq?"

Uto nodded and said "Yes," and her "yes" blended in with the wind like it wanted to listen too.

There was a man named Pisiqsuqliq, which meant "best shooter." He had a camp high in the mountain forest. He could hunt bear, wolf, fox, rabbits, wolverine, and lynx there. He had a tenacious personality—once he went after an animal, he didn't come back until he had gotten it.

He and his wife had their own place. One day, his wife bore him a son. About two years later, she had another son, and then another again after two years. While the sons were about six, eight, and ten years old, Pisiqsuqliq gathered many animal pelts, including a mother bearskin and two young bearskins.

Suddenly, Pisiqsuqliq became sick and died. In those days, when someone died, they didn't bury him in the ground. His two older sons gathered logs and put them in a teepee shape for his burial. The wife and sons wrapped the body in skins. They had a hard time lifting his body onto the log pile.

Spring came and the birds returned and chirped and sang. The wife went to the burial place to mourn for her husband. There she began to hear a bird singing about her husband.

Pisiqsuqliq,
Nuni vee koom,
Pun noa nik,
Nu laa qoaq tuq hoo nee,
Ah na miq na koaq mee hee,
Pisiqsuqliq.

> Where the people get together and spend the
>   winter months,
> There was a young girl there,
> Pisiqsuqliq went and got another wife,
> A young, pretty woman.

The bird continued to sing and the wife got suspicious. It dawned on her that the bird might be singing of the truth, so she climbed up to see whether the body was still there. There was no body.

The wife then soaked the hides of the mother bear and the two young bears, and while she was busy, she thought about how Pisiqsuqliq would never give up when he hunted animals.

She began to train herself to be very fit physically, and when she was strong, she put the mother bearskin on herself and the young bearskins on her two oldest sons. They all could run fast like bears. When she thought they had all trained enough, they walked toward Nunevik.

Someone from that place reported seeing a mother bear with her two cubs. The hunters went after them with bows and arrows, and Pisiqsuqliq was among them. The woman and her two sons were so fit and fast they outran the hunters. Finally, Pisiqsuqliq was alone, still pursuing them. Because of his tenacious personality, his wife knew he would do that.

She and her two sons took the bearskins off. "You want to die and we're going to kill you!" they said. Then they put the bearskins back on and killed him.

The moral of the story is: Don't try to fool your wife.

When Sikki finished her story, both of their sleds were full of the driftwood they had gathered.

Uto said, "Let's sit down and rest before we start back.

"I needed your story today," she told Sikki. "You are my dearest friend, and it makes me sad that you are thinking about death today. So I'm going to tell you a story about life."

Once upon a time, the women of the village wanted the rain to stop. Although it was a rainy summer, they went out to pick salmonberries every day. If they didn't go picking, they knew the berries would get ruined from the rain and they would not have the delicious berries to eat in the winter.

This was the time when all living things could talk to one another. There was a beautiful butterfly who knew only too well that once he was a butterfly, he would not live long enough to see the winter. And he yearned to see the winter.

So when the butterfly heard that the women of the village wanted the rain to stop, he thought he could help them out. All he had to do was fly to where the women were picking salmonberries that day.

At the salmonberry patch, the butterfly noticed two sisters who were the mothers of all the girls. He flew by each girl as she was picking salmon-berries, trying to learn as much about each one of the girls as possible, so he could choose one to help him carry out his plan. He didn't pick the oldest girl because she was already too much like an adult and probably wouldn't believe him. The smaller girls would not yet understand the point of it all. But the girl who was in the middle by age might be willing to try anything, because she loved life, was obedient, and always willing to help out. The butterfly chose her, feeling he had made the right choice.

A little later, this girl happened to wander away down a path where she thought there were more berries. When she heard a tiny voice, she turned around and put her hair behind her ears to hear better. When she heard the voice again, she knew it was real. The voice came closer and closer, and the girl realized the voice was coming from a butterfly that was fluttering around her face. When she held up her hand, it landed on her finger.

The butterfly said to the girl, "If you will help me out, I will make the rain stop."

"What am I to do?" asked the girl.

The butterfly told the girl what to do. "I know that I'm not supposed to turn back into a worm in a cocoon again," he said. "But if I believe hard enough, I will be able to do that." And sure enough, the butterfly turned back into a worm in a cocoon.

The girl looked for a stout grass stem, and proceeded to turn the cocoon inside out with the grass stem. She also started to sing.

If I believe,
And with some help,
It will be done.
The rain will stop,
I will help,
Help save the berries.

Butterfly, have your wish,
Stay awhile,
See the snow.

When Uto finished telling her story, Sikki smiled at her and said, "*Quyana*." She told her friend she was happy now.

"*A ya*!" Sikki exclaimed. "It's time to start home now."

On the walk back, the west wind was behind them, helping them to pull their sleds that were heavy with wood.

10

The Meaning of Qupuk

This morning, Sikki told herself, I have to measure my flour sack salmon net. As she stretched it out, it was almost the length of her little sod house. I hope people will pass on their flour sacks to me, she said to herself. If they do, I will try to make the net twice as long. But I'll be happy with it nevertheless.

On this day, Sikki was singing songs she had learned in church. I think I better start thinking of another project to work on next winter, she thought, as she settled down to work on her net.

Sikki felt happy that she could look forward to the following winter. In the coming spring, she and her friends, the Storytellers, would be out setting their traps that they had traded for at Magid's store. Even before all the snow melted, they would start walking the hills looking for squirrel holes where they would set their traps.

Most of the time, the walks took all day. Sikki didn't know how many traps her friends had, but she had three traps that she had accumulated over the years since they appeared in Magid's store. And she could make more for herself in the old way out of wood and string. Most of the time, she walked the hills with one or two other friends, but sometimes she went by herself, since she didn't have a husband to get back to.

When it was time to set the traps, Sikki put them in her skin backpack that she had sewn. She remembered that her pack needed repairs. As soon as I finish sewing this net, she thought, I'll repair my backpack. The first time out, I'll place the traps in my backpack, and I'll have room for only some water and dry meat. Then probably on the next trip, I or one of my Storyteller friends will bring a pot so we can make a fire and have some tea.

In the hills, Sikki recalled, they worked on skinning the squirrels and cleaning the skins so they wouldn't make trash at home. The scavenger birds had a feast. She and her friends left the guts for the birds but would take home the meat to cook. And the skins they took home would be clean so they could just put them on stretchers.

Squirrel hunting and skin preparation activity lasted for about six weeks in April and May. Sikki thought about how sometimes they would boil some of the meat right there as they worked on skinning the squirrels. The meat was a light meat with a light, stringy texture. It tasted delicious.

The Storytellers would discuss whether each one had enough skins for a parka for a member of her family. When they were satisfied, the skins were stored away in gunnysacks until the summer and fall activities were completed. Then during the dark cold of winter, they would sew the skins into parkas or sleeping bags.

In early spring, the hunters would go out among the icebergs to hunt bearded seal. The men were always excited to begin the hunt for the bearded seal, or *ugruk*. When they got a seal, a hook was put in its mouth and everyone who was there helped pull it up on the grassy part of the beach. The women, children, and dogs all made noise.

Sikki thought about how the women made sure that their *ulus*, or curved knives, were sharpened before the hunters came home. The women who cut up the *ugruk* were experts in cutting up a carcass. First they made a cut under the mouth and then cut all the way down the front. The blubber was then laid to the sides on the grass. Before anything else was done, they went for the intestines. They cleaned those out, washing them in a container of water brought down to the shore. Then the oldest women there would chop the intestine on the blubber that was still attached to the skin. Mmmm, Sikki said to herself. Most everyone enjoyed it.

Also in the spring, the village became a festival of picking all kinds of greens, from *sera*, or willow (*Salix* sp.), to *ikuusuk*, or wild celery (*Heracleum lanatum*); from fireweed, or *kuppikutak* (*Epilobium angustifolium*), to wild rhubarb, or *kunulik* (*Polygonum alaskanum*); from sourdock, or *kuagak* (*Rumex arcticus*), to Hudson's Bay tea (also called Labrador tea), or *tilaakik* (*Ledum decumbens*); and so on. Once they brought the greens home, it was important to allow the leaves to rest and cool before they preserved them in fresh seal oil from the spring hunt. Sikki thought, it's like allowing the greens to have a grieving time before their spirits succumb.

At the same time that greens were being picked, Sikki reminisced, it was duck-hunting time. It was the time to go after eggs, and to relish hot duck broth. It was also a time of new hope, because the geese, cranes, and ducks were having their young, and then they flew south in the fall, and returned again in the spring.

When that activity was done, everyone was happy, and grateful as the berries began to ripen in the summer, she thought. The people then became busy picking berries. In the village of Ipnatchiaq, the women always went out on August 9, when Ayi gave the signal to all women of the village. That way, everyone had an equal chance at the luscious *akpik*, or salmonberry (*Rubus chamaemorus*). Everything was shared among them, even unpicked salmonberries.

Summer was also the season when the salmon returned to the river. Everyone—men, women, and children—seemed to be the busiest then. The people either had a set net a little way up the river that they checked every day, or they would seine with a net off the shore. Sikki said to herself, I can't wait to set my net up the river, where I can take my little boat and row back and forth. Walter and I will be doing this.

And finally, Sikki thought, it will be September, when we harvest cranberries, or *kikminak* (*Vaccinium vitis-idaea*). That time is the best time to be outdoors, looking at this Great Land before it becomes all covered with snow again. The bugs are less bothersome and the land takes on red and yellow colors. It is also the best time to be eating cranberries, because they relieve the headaches and sore throats that seem to come around that time of year.

Then, Sikki thought, we will have one more great fishing period—ice fishing for tomcod. I'll be ready then to begin working on the squirrel skin parka I'll sew for myself. When I make my parka, I will start with the pattern that is around the bottom just above the wolverine trim. Since I was my husband's only wife, I will be making two rounds of pattern.

And with that thought, Sikki began to think about a story that her cousin Qutla had told her.

Qutla's biological father was a man from Seelvik. He became an excellent hunter and because of that, he could support four wives. Qutla's mother, Paneluq, had been his first wife, so she was called the *nulakpunqa*. She was also known as the pot maker. His second wife

was Kalayuq, and the name of his third wife was
Ahgayaq. The fourth wife was Napoktuq. They were
called *nukakuq.*

This man thought that he could support another
wife. Her name was Atolhuq. She was very young and
was another beautiful girl. When her father found
out that his daughter was about to become this man's
fifth wife, he immediately went to her and brought
her back home.

After that, the whole family unit disintegrated.
All the wives started new lives, with other husbands.
They all established strong families. Paneluq started life
again with Mungnuk as her second husband, and they
had one child named Nuyaqik. Mungnuk also took
Qutla as his own, and treated her with fatherly love
until his death.

Of all the stories ever told, and I have heard a lot of
them, Qutla's story after her father died is the most
horrifying one I have ever heard, Sikki thought to
herself. Some day I may be able to share it with the
other Storytellers. But I will wait until I am ready to
tell the story in a way that gives her the honor she
deserves after her life's struggle. I am in awe of her,

and I felt it once again when she and Egaq were just here for a visit.

Then Sikki began thinking about making her parka again. She thought about how, just a generation before hers when there was no brightly colored cotton fabric like they used now, the women made their "public" parkas out of fur. They used a black material to outline the rows at the bottom of the parka, which was made from the skin of a black fish that had a smile like a puppy. Sikki did not know what the fish was called in the English language, but it was *gayoulouk* in Inupiaq. In the old days, the rows along the lower edge of the parka were made of light brown caribou skin with only a light layer of hair. Sikki would have two rows of caribou skin, with three rows of the black material, one above the top row of caribou skin, one below the top row, and then one in the middle at the bottom. *Qupuk* is the word for this trim pattern on the bottom of the parka and also at the top of the *mukluks.*

As far as I know, Sikki said to herself, Qutla's mother, Paneluq, would also show two strips of caribou skin, since she was first the primary wife to the man from Seelvik. And if that family unit had continued, Kalayuq, Ahgayaq, and Napoktuq would have one strip of the light-colored caribou skin at the bottom of their parkas, outlined with black fish skin. But since they had moved on and started their own family units, each would also have two strips outlined with the black material. Sikki continued to be deep in thought as she sat there, weaving her net.

11

At Uto's House

As Uto's friends came one by one into her home—the house that was built for Miss Stratton, the missionary—she greeted each one graciously. After all the Storytellers were seated in their usual places and everyone was served tea, Uto began to talk.

"Before we get started, I just want to say this to my friends. Every day I'm thankful to be back in our own village also, just like Sikki. I love to hear my grandchildren, George and Jean, playing outside with Walter, their friend. I love everything that comes with living by the ocean. I just wanted my Storytelling friends to know how happy and thankful I feel today.

"So," Uto continued, "today we will share in our normal way. But we will talk about what we think is important in our lives—how we can get along better. We won't draw today.

"I know that a sense of humor is important to each of us. We should never forget to promote humor in our lives," Uto said. "We need to teach our children to seek out their own sense of humor, because it is good to laugh, not at people but with them. And tell your children to remember to laugh at themselves once in a while, so they can grow up to be happier people. And when they become great, they can laugh and share happiness with people around them.

"Every person in our village who has held a small baby or a small child has experienced the power of gentleness," Uto continued. "When we were in our child-bearing years, we focused more on how much work was involved in taking care of our babies than sitting back and enjoying the feeling of gentleness that comes from them and from within ourselves when we are with them. It's only when we become grandparents that we realize that we, too, are capable of a God-given gentleness, and then we give thanks.

"I have a little story about sharing, which to me is the reason our culture survives, Uto said. "It is perhaps one of the most important values that we live out every day. As women in our society, we no longer have to worry that we will become beggars when our husbands die. Sharing gives us reassurance that our people will take care of us with the food we need to live. Sharing allows us to keep our dignity and our place in our village of Ipnatchiaq."

And so Uto began to tell her story.

Once there were *inuguluurak,* or little people, who were about two feet in stature. They were not dwarfs, but were proportionate small human beings. They spoke Inupiaq.

At one time before the white people arrived, there were an *inuguluurak* man, woman, and child living in Ipnatchiaq. They had lived here for quite some time. One day a dog killed their child. They packed up and left. No one knows where they went.

There was a hunter who was going after caribou up the Nuataaq River. While he was butchering caribou by himself, he heard someone speak to him with a customary greeting. He turned around and didn't see anything, so he went back to his work.

A little man appeared, dressed in skin clothing, with a bow and arrow. He asked the hunter, "May I have that caribou head?"

"Sure, you may have it," replied the hunter.

So the little man tied the head up, pulled it up on his back, and packed it away. To where? No one knows. But the lesson of this story is that our people always share whatever they have no matter where they are.

Uto continued. "The new value I assigned myself is called 'preventing hostility.' One big way that we can avoid conflict is to not take anything that's not ours, whether it's a wife, a husband, children, or any material thing. I believe that whatever we do will also be done to us in our lifetime.

"Our lifestyle is becoming more like the white people's lifestyle, with one man and one woman together. If we accept that, we should teach our children to honor that.

"And lastly," Uto said, "I believe that we should not fool anyone, especially those who love us. In the end, we only fool ourselves."

Because the Storytellers sat in the same places in each house, Sikki began speaking without cue.

"In just our lifetime," she said, "compassion has taken the place of the taboos we used to have to observe. I know I often talk about the woman whose name is Qutleruq—Qutla, my cousin. When she was a small girl, the *aŋatkuḳ,* or shaman, advised the family not to braid anything or else the father would die. His death was blamed on Qutla, because she braided grass while she was playing with her friends on the beach. After that, she became an outcast by the people of the village, including her mother who told her it should have been Qutla whose breath was taken away. But after years of hardship, she became the one, along with Miss Hunnicutt, the white missionary, to administer the teachings of Jesus to her people. And so, the people slowly replaced taboos with compassion, a value that we cherish today.

"We also show respect for others through our hard work," Sikki went on. "In our life, nothing is easy. And because we all know what it takes to acquire everything we have, we have respect for others. There's nothing more to add to those two important principles we live by.

"And the last value I want to talk about is patience," Sikki said. "Having patience is one of the hardest qualities to possess because we tend to want something immediately. We must teach patience by encouragement—that eventually we will learn how to do something by practicing and practicing.

"Having patience can save one's life. For example, when the pack ice breaks from shore, never try to get ashore where the water is deep. If you have patience, the water currents will bring you back to shore. And now, as grandmothers, with our children grown and gone, sometimes we wish life was like it was when they were home. But when you give of yourself to your family, the children and grandchildren will always come home. Be patient."

Uto told the storytellers to take a break while she checked the reindeer soup she was cooking. She cheerfully anticipated the delicious soup she would share with her Storytelling friends.

When everyone was back and seated, Ne started her contribution for that day.

~~~~~~~

"The values that we live by," Ne began, "such as love, love for children, respect for elders, and cooperation, are what I'm going to talk about today.

"We all love our families. Some of our marriages were arranged by our parents and in some cases our marriages didn't begin with love. But as we experienced life with our partners, love grew. Since the missionaries and the miners arrived, our young people have begun choosing their own partners because they say they're in love. I say that is better than being forced to have someone for a partner.

"Our love for children has changed too. The missionaries taught us that it wasn't a good practice to get rid of our girl babies even in times of hardship. As we all know, girl babies grow up to be people like us. Our ancestors loved their babies, but I feel that things were done because of life-or-death circumstances such as what happened to Ayi's cousin Qutuq, who lives in Kuuyuk. I'm happy that the life of a woman in our society is getting easier. We're not bound by the *aŋatkuk's* rules anymore.

"As for respect for elders," Ne continued, "that is getting better also. A long time ago, elders were often left behind in times of scarce food. Now we tell our young people to take care of the elders because they are taking care of our history. It doesn't matter how the elders may have lived their lives. We still must take care of them.

"And most of us are not interested in becoming the most liked person or the most important. We just want to be important to our own families, because in the end, we want to leave them with good memories.

"And lastly, there is cooperation. We all help one another in gathering food, in raising children, and in living by the rules of nature—without greed."

And with that, all the Storytellers clapped their hands and exclaimed, "*Akomae*!"

Nupa began to talk with a "*Kuyanak*" and a short prayer that she was known for. "I hope I can do as well as Ne.

"I'll start with spirituality. As a people, we have always known about the spirit. We call it *ilitkusik*. Before the missionaries came, we believed that everything had a spirit. We were afraid to make anything angry, such as the sea or the sky or the animals. Now, we have switched to just one God, or *Atunik*, who is the master of everything. It is better that way.

"At this time in our lives, helping each other is something I prize, for without the help of each one of you, life would not be as good. We need to keep talking about this to our children and so they can help one another like we do. Not only helping with all the game that we hunt and prepare, but we also need to pass on the importance of storytelling. It helps to teach the young, gives them imagination, and hopefully they will strive to live better lives.

"I know that we six women of the village of Ipnatchiaq have created this bond as Storytellers. But we need to encourage all the women of the village to be included, and their daughters also. So someday, if they no longer live here, they and their children will forever say that they are from the village of Ipnatchiaq.

"Also I would like to thank Ayi for reminding us to respect everyone and all things in our village life. Each person owns this respect, but sometimes we need to be reminded of how important it is. When we set our seal nets in the fall, everyone knows where his or her place is to set the nets, and no one questions that authority. This is called respect for humans, animals, property, and land. To this, I will add respect for the sea. I thank you for listening to how I think things used to be, how they are now, and our dreams for the future."

Ayi cleared her throat, because it was her turn. She smiled at Ne and acknowledged what was said about her.

"I want to first talk about humility. It's not that I am displeased with these comments. I feel honored. But I think what we need to pass on to our children is this: Even if you think you are important, you are not important if you act like you're better than others. The one who thinks he or she is important is just making a fool of himself or herself, because the rest of us know the truth. We need to tell our children to smile like I just smiled and acknowledged Ne.

"In our village, we have what's called 'hunter success,'" Ayi continued. "We need to remind our hunters never to boast about what great hunters they've become. Someone else will boast for them, and it is better that way.

"Along with that, we also prize the value of endurance. And when competition is accepted by all, like during the games we play, it is okay to show what endurance you have. My dream is for our young people to have an endurance race that begins in our village of Ipnatchiaq and ends in another village. That would create some fantastic tales and might restore pride among our young people. I would equate it with the endurance of the three giants who lived here so long ago.

"We also need to teach our young to have a responsibility to our generations," Ayi said. "They should show this by first being honest with themselves, and trying never to be someone they are not. It is important to never forsake our culture, but to be proud of where we come from. I say this because some of our people are now marrying into the white culture and we don't know much about that culture yet."

Uto announced, "Let's take a break." And all the Storytellers got up and went out.

Uto checked the stove, put in more wood, and then put a pan of biscuits in the oven. She thought, by the time Panea is through speaking, my biscuits will be ready.

When the women returned and were seated again, Panea began to speak.

"Today I am the last one to tell you my thoughts. I am so happy to be with you today. The values I want to talk about are friendship, family relationship roles, domestic skills, and avoiding mockery.

"The first value is friendship. We are friends, but we need to extend this group to all the women of the village, like Ne said. I think if we do that, we can all learn more about one another.

"About family relationships and roles," Panea said, "I want to tell you something that I told Qutla when she was just here with her husband, Egaq. I tried to have a Native man as my husband, but we did not do very well. So my husband now is a full-blood Japanese man named George. I call him Yoneruq. I feel that you shouldn't have to be with someone if you are not happy.

"Along with my husband, there were two other Japanese men who came to our village at the same time. Their names were Charlie Okuda and Harry Nakamura. They chose to become part of our lives— becoming husbands and having children.

"We all know the importance of domestic skills," Panea continued. "We all work very hard, or our families would go without. We need to teach our children not to be lazy. Here in the North Country, there's no room for a lazy person. For us, it would be an embarrassment, because we know that when a lazy person isn't working, the burden goes on another member of the family. And the people know that he or she is a scapegoat, taking the blame for the lazy ones. As parents, we always tried to prevent that happening among our children, but in some cases we didn't succeed.

"We all tried to be good parents, but sometimes our children mock others, especially when we're not watching them. We need to continually tell them never to make fun of anyone, male or female, who is different. We believe that when we make fun of someone, we will have a child with those traits. Likewise children should not make fun of someone who doesn't speak like a normal person, or someone who walks with a limp, or someone who is cross-eyed. And tell your children never to laugh at women who are not very pretty or at men who have a hard time getting a wife. The list goes on and on.

"*Adee*," Panea said, with a sigh. "I'm going to stop speaking of that side of our lives now. Sometimes we have to discuss our values to help us live better lives. I thank you for listening to me and for being my friends."

And so, Uto said, "I invite you, my friends, to have dinner before you go back home. My husband and grandchildren and Sikki's grandson Walter will join us. Let's eat!"

12

Walter's Future

"Bye, grandma," Walter said. "I'm going to walk to school with my friends." And then he was out the door.

Sikki put her parka on, and went outside to watch him walking toward his school friends. While she was outside, she could hear dogs in the village barking. "I wonder where they're traveling to today," Sikki thought.

When the Storytellers recently met at Uto's home, four of them had brought their empty flour sacks for Sikki. On this day, after Walter was at school and the ice and wood had been brought in, Sikki sat down at her window and began to unravel the flour sacks and turn the thread into a ball of red, white, and blue string.

She occasionally looked out her window, which faced south. Everything was white, and it was easy for her thoughts to flow. She began thinking about how just a few weeks ago she had walked her grandson to school, and about how he was now confident enough to walk to school by himself. He seemed to be growing up so fast in the short time since he had come to live with her. Today I feel worried about his future, she thought.

Sikki recalled that when she was young, she seldom saw people from another culture. Her mother, Ekiyuq, was half white, and she told Sikki the shipwreck story of white people who came from far away. Ekiyuq said they had seen many ships sailing north in the summertime. Then in the winter, her people were mostly left to themselves, to live through the seasons.

Sikki remembered that after she and Utli were married and their three children were young people, gold miners began arriving. That's when barge after barge with mining equipment came to their small village of Ipnatchiaq. The miners needed a road to the gold mine, so some men of the village worked on building the road. That had been the first time the villagers set eyes on certain machinery such as the trucks that went back and forth, up the river to the gold mine.

Sikki thought, I should make myself some tea and put more wood in the stove.

Once she was back sitting on the caribou skin on the floor, looking out at the white winter landscape and unraveling her flour sack, she said to herself, I hope Walter is listening to the teacher, Mr. Tony Joule. When I saw Mr. Joule at Magid's store, he told me that Walter and a couple of his little friends tried to take some pencils through an open window at school. He said he had hit Walter's hand with a ruler to prevent him from taking the pencils. He told me that the boys didn't need to steal pencils. If they asked him for the pencils, he would gladly give them each a pencil. I hope that Walter will remember this all of his life and won't try to steal anything else.

Sikki continued with her thoughts. A long time ago before the white miners began coming in the summertime, our little village of Ipnatchiaq operated under a chief. I can't remember his name anymore. It's as if that life of long ago were just a dream, and it bothers me that I don't remember his name. When I visit with my Storytelling friends, I'm sure one of them will recall his name.

I remember how strong and confident our chief was. How the other men around him would seek his advice on everyday tasks or with the more important decisions that had to be made for the good of the village. That's what I'm missing in my grandson's life, she thought. I would like Walter to be in the presence of a man like that. I remember that our young boys had dreams of becoming like the chief. He was not only a great hunter and knew everything about the animals, the land, and the sky, but he had a certain presence about him. He had worked hard all his life to become that person. I was proud of him even though he was not in my family. He made everyone in the village feel safe.

In those days, Sikki recalled, they had a *qasgi* where the chief and all the men of the village spent much of their time. The chief was a trusted guide for the young men and they were devoted to him in return. How Sikki wished that Walter could have that kind of mentoring while she was still alive. She could wish it, but at the same time she knew it would not happen. She had seen that custom taken away when their village had been moved up north.

The young boys, she reminisced, were once cherished to the point of spoiling them. They were treated that way because they were destined to be keepers of the tradition. Their goals in life would be channeled by the old men of the village. The young boys in turn paid attention to the elders because they knew they were being taught everything they needed to know in order to be successful in their lives.

Sikki thought about the school her grandson attended. The biggest difference in what was being taught there was that the children did not use what they learned there when they came home.

When our young boys learned at the *qasgi*, she remembered, we could really see what they learned. First they studied how to make the tools, sleds, and boats needed for the hunt. Then sometime later in their lives, we as mothers sewed clothes for them that were just like their father's clothes. I'm sure that made them feel special. As far as I know, she thought to herself, the young boys were given all they needed by the elders of the village to continue to be the keepers of our subsistence tradition. All the women needed to do was feed and clothe them. The old men included in their teaching all that was important to us in our culture, she recalled, like the values that the Storytellers talked about at Uto's home.

Now since we do not have the *qasgi* anymore, Sikki told herself, it is up to me to teach Walter everything that is important to us. I don't feel I can do all that. This is 1925 and I'm forty-six years old now and Walter is six years old. Maybe his mother, Ruby, and Walter's father, Murphy Eterorock, will soon come back to Ipnatchiaq to live and raise him, she thought.

Then Sikki put down the red, white, and blue ball of string and got up. She put on her parka and went outside to bring in more wood. While she was outside, her neighbor Frank Henry, the miner, waved to her and she waved back.

Back at her window, as she ripped her last flour sack to work on a ball of string, Sikki was still worrying about Walter. She began thinking about her Storytelling friends and how they meet and help one another. That's what the old men in the *qasgi* had, she thought. They had a support system for all the males born into the village. They were responsible for the well-being of each and every male. Each young boy had all the attention he needed, and all he needed to do was grow up and become a contributing member of society, following the rules and guidance he had received.

I wish the old men of the village would begin such a group, she thought, for the common purpose of making sure every male in the village had a support system. These days, it would have to include the *naluagmiu,* or white men, because they now live among us. But that would be a good thing, because they could teach our young men some things about the ways of the *naluagmiu*. Hopefully, our young men will choose the good from that culture.

My Storytelling friends and I have already seen what *tannak*, or alcohol, can do to our people, Sikki thought. That's one bad thing the *naluagmiu* brought. I hope Walter won't choose that way of life. And we learned from the missionary here that to drink *tannak* is a sin. They have said that smoking is a sin also. So what we are becoming in the village are the Christians and the sinners. The missionaries have changed our lives for the better because they are doing away with the taboos in our lives, especially those having to do with childbirth. But I really can't understand why they label some activities as sins. The missionaries say that if we do those things, we will go to their Hell. Some of our people do not understand this Hell. They prefer to drink and smoke instead.

Some of my children drink and smoke, Sikki thought, but I will not believe that they will go to the *naluagmiu*'s Hell. I love them too much. My oldest daughter, Topsy, got married to a white man. His last name is Swanson. I like him because he adopted one of Ruby's little boys, Ralph. He wants to take care of the boy, so that makes him a good person in my opinion.

When I meet with my Storytelling friends, she said to herself, I will bring up the subject of their husbands starting up a mentoring program for our young boys, which was crushed when the missionaries arrived in our region and the gold miners established their supply station for the Interior Gold Mine in 1901.

I heard that up north, they call us "the remnant culture." To me that means "what is left." They called our village *Ipnatchiaqmiut*, which means "people of Ipnatchiaq." We are the Malemiut Inupiat living by the Ipnatchiaq River. I want us to become proud of our ways again even if we are called a remnant culture. To do that, we have to rediscover how we used to treat one another with respect, but at the same time, adopt the good things of the *naluagmiu* culture. That's what I want my grandson Walter to consider, Sikki said.

13

At Ayi's House

"Since there's not much room in my house, we will not all draw everyone's picture like we usually do," Ayi announced after the Storytellers were seated. "First, let's have some tea, and then each of us will draw her own picture. These indelible pencils take so much work to make a mark. Every time I get home, my family laughs at me because my lips are black—just like a dead person, they say."

The Storytellers had a good laugh and nodded their heads in agreement.

"Okay," Ayi said, "everyone has a pencil, a cup of tea, and some paper. Just draw one thing from the story you are going to tell. Since it's just one thing, we won't work so hard and it won't take us so long. We will show our drawings to each other when we each speak. Okay, start drawing."

After about ten or fifteen minutes, Ayi told them to stop. "Today," she said, "I'm not going to tell a story like your stories. Your stories are for teaching our children and our young people some things about life. What I will do today is talk about each one of you. I will start with Panea."

Ayi turned to her left to face Panea and said, "Panea, you are a good woman. I've seen you share everything that you have with the young couples around you. You must know some things we don't know. When you were young, you probably wished that someone would treat you with generosity like you treat people today. Thank you so much for your kindness. And since you are seated to my left, you will start."

Panea smiled, and without hesitating, she began her story.

I knew a young mother once who told me some-thing that I will never forget. She came to my home and asked if she could confide in me. When I told her that I would be happy to help her, she made me promise never to tell anyone her name. It would be okay to talk about what she was going to tell me if it would help others, but I could not mention her name.

So she told me to follow her. We went outside and she pointed toward Evelequruq Creek. "Tell your family we're going to look for berries way up the creek," she said, "and you'll be gone for three or four hours. Tell them that so they won't worry."

As we walked, the young woman told her story. When the gold miners arrived near the village of Ipnatchiaq in 1901, her mother was one of the young women the Natives talk about in a bad way. The mother told her how bad she had felt her whole life for straying from the rules of their culture. It seemed easy to do that because she began to drink firewater with a gold miner. After she became involved with the gold miner, the young man who she was to marry did not want her anymore. So she began to take this walk that we are on now.

Her mother told her how demeaning she felt her life had become, as if a mark was on her telling everybody how bad she was. This young person was going to walk until she couldn't walk anymore. No one liked her anymore, she felt.

The young woman told me, "We will walk until we reach the base of the little hill about a mile back. I was curious what she wanted to show me. As I was looking, I didn't notice anything out of the ordinary. It was a tough walk through the tussocks. Sometimes there was water we had to jump across. We were following our creek, Evelequruq.

When we reached the little hill, there was a smaller creek, about two feet wide in some places. It was easy to jump across.

"Don't be afraid and just do what I do," the young woman said. She knelt down on one knee and I did the same. Then she put her hand in the creek to let the water rush over her hand, and I did it too. We both became needlefish, just like those that live in the little creek. Although we were fish, we could talk to each other. She told me her mother had turned into a needlefish when she felt like there was a mark on her telling people how bad she was. And that if you look up on the sides of the little creek, you will see everything you have done in your life so far.

Sure enough, as the stream carried us away, I could watch my life play out, beginning when I was born.

I saw my parents taking care of me after my mother returned from the birthing place. I remembered how much they loved me.

The young woman wanted to show me what her mother had gone through. So we watched her as a baby, then as a little girl, then as a teenager when the gold miners arrived. We watched her mother drinking with the gold miner. We saw how it had changed her into a different person. Before that happened, everyone had loved her and had looked up to her.

The young mother then warned me that something was going to come around the bend of the creek. That in everyone's life, no matter how far down the creek you wanted to go, something chases you back. And you have to fight hard against the current of the creek for your self-esteem.

The young mother told me that her mother had almost been eaten by a bullhead living in Evelequruq Creek. She fought and swam so hard that it erased the part of her life that she was ashamed of. Her mother was teaching her to fight back, to fight for what is good. Fight for yourself, and ultimately the bad memories will be washed down the stream to be eaten by a bullhead.

"And this is my picture," Panea said, as she held up her picture.

Panea's bullhead fish [DRAWING BY LORETTA OUTWATER COX]

~~~~~~~~

Ayi thanked her, and said, "We'll have one more story before we take our break. I want to tell you about Uto. If I could choose my mother, I would've chosen Uto. She and her husband have made a good home for their children. They are always teaching them the ways of our culture. Okay, Uto, this is your time."

Uto began to speak about rock climbing for eggs.

The name of our bluff is Kippalu. Every spring, my family and I look forward to eating a diet of eggs. So we plan for it beginning in the fall when we set out our seal nets. From the seal hides, my husband and I make *aleq*, for a whole week it seems. Just as when people bring their empty flour sacks to Sikki, people bring their leftover seal hides to us because they know we will make *aleq* from them. Then no matter how many or how few eggs my family and I get from the cliffs, we share them with the people who brought us seal hides.

We make the same kind of *aleq* the two giants used when one of them walked on it out to the big rock that sticks out of the ocean near Kippalu. First we *ute* the skin by letting it soak in a container of water in the house; *ute* means to let the hair fall off. Then we take great care to cut the pieces of skin a certain width so the *aleq* will be strong enough to hold our rock climbers. Then to make the *aleq* as long as we need it, my husband and I sew the ends together with sinew. We use a stitch called a double-stitch to connect the ends so that the rawhide rope is as strong as if it were one piece.

When the time comes to go and rock climb for eggs, two of my sons and two or three other young men get up early. Sometimes they even stay awake all night like young people do in the spring, but we encourage them to get some sleep because climbing down the cliff is dangerous. Then my husband and I take the ocean-going boat and row down to the bluff, or sail there if a breeze is blowing from the right direction. We are careful not to go when it's too windy, though, because the waves will be too rough. The young men meet us at the bluff, up on top.

When our boat is in the right position below the cliff, two climbers rappel down the cliff to us.

"*Eeee!*" I can hear myself say. It is awesome to watch the young men on their ropes, so unafraid. I don't ask my sons to do it if they are afraid. That would be inviting trouble. As the climbers make their way down the cliff, they gather eggs from the bird nests.

Once they reach our boat at the bottom, they hand papa and me the eggs. Then some strong young men at the top pull them back up, one at a time. Then they rappel down again, picking up more eggs. When we are collecting eggs, the people in Ipnatchiaq can hear all the noise coming from the birds screeching at Kippalu.

I told you that before we do this egg gathering activity, we encourage our young men to get enough sleep. They need to have clear minds when they are coming down the cliff. One time, one of my sons did not listen to us. He stayed up all night, but we didn't know it. I thought I could scold my kids when I have to. But you should have heard an eider duck scold one of my sons when he dropped an egg into the ocean.

When this happened, I looked at papa and he looked at me. We each thought the other was scolding our son through this bird's noise. By the time our son reached the boat, he looked at us and said he would never stay up all night again before picking eggs off the cliff.

~~~~~~~

Uto's eider duck [DRAWING BY LORETTA OUTWATER COX]

Ayi told the Storytellers that it was time to take a short break.

When everyone was back and seated again, Ayi turned to Sikki. "We never know what's in our future," she said. "Sikki didn't know that her daughter Ruby wouldn't be ready to return to our village when Sikki went up north to bring her back home. Instead, Ruby needed help with her son Walter, so Sikki is raising him now. Even as grandmothers, we are happy to help with our families. She is setting a good example for all of us."

Everyone looked at Sikki, and she started her story.

Living here in Ipnatchiaq, we're used to the winter storms that we have every year. When we're in the village, we're not afraid to go about our business because we know which direction to walk to reach our destination. All of us feel safe, even in the worst snow storm.

Once my grandson Emuk was walking home from school. His English name is Walter, but for this story, I'll use his Inupiaq name, Emuk. He and other children who live uptown were walking home together. One by one everyone went into their houses until only Emuk was left to continue walking home where I was waiting. The parents had faith in their children's ability to get home, even in a storm—that's just the way it is.

In the area where he had to walk back from the seashore to the Ipnatchiaq River, the blizzard was as thick as *akutuq* in my wooden mixing bowl, Walter told me, once he tumbled in the door.

I asked him, "What did you do?"

He told me that the sky above him swirled around him in white feathers, and he could only see our house in the distance for one second here and there. Then the snow got so thick that he just sat on the snowy ground. Everything happened so fast and the white snowflakes were moving around him so thickly that he forgot to be afraid. He could only see white air around him. He said it felt like he was floating, but he knew he was sitting on the ground.

Emuk told me that then a woman appeared to him, who said, "Don't be afraid. I've been watching and taking care of you your whole life." She then asked him, "If you had a wish, what would you wish for?"

He said the woman made him feel so unafraid, it wasn't hard to answer her question. He told her he wished to become a great hunter some day, like the *kayaq* hunters at Elephant Point who herd the beluga whales into shallow water. The woman told him that she approved of his wish.

She also said that she knew there were times when he wished that his mother and father were with him, like Uto's children, his friends, who lived with both their parents.

She also told him to treat everyone the same, that no one is better than the others.

Emuk told Sikki that the magical woman also told him that his wish would come true. When he grew up, he would become a great hunter. She said in the future when he became a great hunter, he would have only one wife. Things such as husbands with more wives or ways of the *aŋatkuk̲s* would disappear. And his wife would be called Kenaq, and she would be well suited to him. They would work hard together to make a good life for themselves and for their children.

Emuk remembered one last thing the magical woman told him: he would live a long life and there would be many in his family. So every time he became lonesome for his own mother and father, she said he should instead look forward to the future and imagine all his descendants around him.

~~~~~~~

Sikki's beluga whales [DRAWING BY LORETTA OUTWATER COX]

Ayi then turned to Ne, and said, "One of our favorite women is Ne. She loves to cook for her family, and her home always smells good when I go to visit her. Ne, tell us your story."

And so Ne began to speak.

Once there was a little girl who was about nine years old. Her name was Ekiyuq. As she was growing up, she became more and more independent. She loved to venture out in the village of Ipnatchiaq. She and about ten other children played together.

One day after dinner, Ekiyuq asked her mother if she could go out to play after she was through clearing the table. Her mother told her not to go too far because it was getting dark.

Instead of finding her friends, Ekiyuq decided to walk toward the bluff by herself. She knew there was a yellow substance found around the rocks. "I'll get some so my friends and I can use it to play house with. We can make pancakes," she thought. In her home, the art of making pancakes was new and her family loved to eat them.

On and on she walked, but she could not reach the place where she had noticed the yellow substance.

"I know there are no animals here except for mice and birds," she told herself, to keep up her courage. And she kept walking.

Finally she reached the rocks where she thought the yellow powder was. It took her some effort to climb up the rocks. As she climbed, she could see the huge rock that stuck up in the ocean with the top larger than the bottom. That's where the two giants were, and one tried to kill the other, Ekiyuq thought, as she remembered the story. She could imagine one of the giants standing at the top of the rock and his brother cutting the *aleq* so that his brother would die. Just as she was thinking that, she spotted the yellow powdery substance.

Now what will I use to bring the yellow powder back home? thought the little girl. Since she didn't have a container, she found a stick and began to play with the yellow powder. She lost track of time since she was so fascinated with the yellow substance. As she dug the powder, a pile of it grew. Then she began to get sleepy, so she stretched out on the edge of the rocks where the ground was mossy and dry, and fell asleep.

When an ocean breeze hit her face, she opened her eyes. Oh, where am I? she thought. It was dark, and she remembered her mother telling her not to go too far.

How am I going to climb down these rocks in the dark? Ekiyuq asked herself, trying not to panic.

"Put some of that yellow powder in your *atige*, or cloth parka, pocket," a voice said to her. "And don't be afraid. Look up toward the sky and look at me. I am the moon."

As Ekiyuq looked up, she could see the man in the moon smiling.

The voice said again, "Put some of the yellow powder in your pocket so that I can help you climb down the rocks."

In the dark, she dropped to the ground to find the pile of yellow powder. Once she found it, she scooped it up with her hands and filled her *atige* pocket. Once her pocket was full, she stood up and looked at the moon. As she looked, a bright shimmery line moved from her pocket to the moon. Ekiyuq blinked her eyes.

Once the shimmery line reached the moon, the moon said, "I am holding your hand. Just take your steps and I will guide you."

Once Ekiyuq was safely down off the rocks, she looked up at the moon and said, "Thank you. What shall I call you?"

"My name is Takkik," answered the moon. "Your ancestors gave me that name before anyone else gave

Ne's moon [Drawing by Loretta Outwater Cox]

me a name. I hate the name that the *naluagmiu* gave me—'moon.'"

He laughed and asked Ekiyuq, "Could I give you my name?"

"No, I like my name," Ekiyuq answered.

"Now hold the line," Takkik said, "and I will walk home with you. You can see my reflection on the ocean."

Ayi told the Storytellers to stand up and take a break. It felt so good when they stood up and stretched. Then they went outside.

When they got back, Ayi said, "Thank you for all your good stories. Now Nupa will tell us the last story for today."

Ayi continued, "I also want to say, Nupa, that we the women of Ipnatchiaq have been privileged with your presence. Watching you make *mukluks* is like watching an excellent artist, and we strive to be like you. Tell us your story, Nupa."

And so Nupa began to speak.

Once upon a time, there was a family who moved to another village because they wanted to be near their elderly parents to help them. The couple had eight children. In times past, there were whispers of what might've been done to elderly people when times were hard. But since the missionaries brought new beliefs, one of them being to honor your father and mother, they didn't question whether they were doing the right thing.

After moving to the new village, this family was welcomed by the people. It was easy for them to slip into their cycle of life, gathering food for the winter months.

When summer arrived, they all got ready to go to the fish camp across the bay. It was so much fun for all the children to be taken by boat on the big open water. This family loved the summertime, its smells and sounds.

As they traveled on the bay, a seagull landed on the bow of their boat and spoke to them. "Since you were not selfish with your time and came here to help your elderly parents, we seagulls will give you all the help that we can. While you are on the open water, we will warn you if there is a storm coming."

And just as the gull announced that, he flew up into the air as if nothing had happened. The family also went about the business of traveling on the ocean, and each wondered if what they had seen really happened. No one said anything about the seagull.

Toward evening, when they arrived at the first camp where they would stay for a few days, the children first helped unload the boat. Some of the older children helped set up the tent, and some helped gather wood to make a fire so the evening meal could be cooked.

After everything was done and the mother was cooking the meal, the children ran to play and explore around the nearby lakes, with one of the older sisters keeping watch over them. They loved chasing the ducks, which always flew away. They all laughed and had a lot of fun.

When everyone was in bed for the night and almost asleep, they heard loons calling on the lakes. One of the loons said, "We like the family who moved here from a village up north to help their elderly parents. We saw how the children played and listened to the older sister. We will help take care of the children. We will tell our friends the salmon to give them help if they need it."

No one in the family moved or said anything. They all went to sleep wondering whether they had imagined hearing those things.

The next day was a beautiful one, with just enough wind to keep the mosquitoes away. The

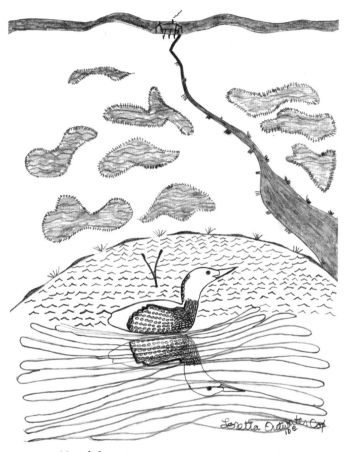

Nupa's loon [DRAWING BY LORETTA OUTWATER COX]

mother told the children, "Go ahead and take a swim in the river."

The younger children didn't go, but the three older sisters went.

They looked across the narrow river toward a sandbar. "Let's go to the sandbar," said one of the older sisters. But as the three started toward it, the river-bank beneath the water made a sudden drop and they began to sink. Two of the girls were able to make it back to shore after panicking and swirling their arms about in the water. The third girl's head went under, and the other girls could only see her hand above the water because the water was so silty.

But soon she appeared, walking along the bottom as if the riverbank weren't giving way under her. A salmon had helped bring her to shallow water.

"There you are," said the salmon, as its head skimmed the top of the water. Then he swam away.

Ayi smiled at everyone and told the Storytellers to look at each other's lips. "Today, since we haven't used our pencils so much," she said, "we don't look like we're dead." And everyone laughed.

14

Happy in Ipnatchiaq

After the first year of helping Walter go to school, Sikki knew that she could not do that the next year. I loved those years, taking care of my little grandson, she recalled fondly. Those were times when I could still do a lot of my own work with the help of my Storytelling friends, she remembered. I hated to admit to myself that age limits what your body can do, especially when activities have to be repeated daily. My mind was willing, but my body was not. So I asked myself, what was better for my grandson Walter?

Sikki decided to ask her friend in the village, who had come from Qigiqtaq (Shismaref), named Bessie

Barr, if one of her children would adopt Walter. Sikki felt that he needed younger parents who could help him learn the ways of hunting and also help him go to school every day. It was agreed that Fanny Barr would adopt Walter in the Native way, which meant that she would just take him in.

Walter lived with the Barrs for about two years. Sikki was grateful that he was being raised by young people who took good care of him. She remembered that when she visited them, she noticed that Walter was learning how to speak their Native dialect. She thought it was good that he would know two dialects.

Sikki often wondered whether her grandson was happy changing families. She would never forget how she had bonded with Walter and how she sometimes forgot that he wasn't her own baby. She felt so protective of him, just like one of her own, and she would sometimes wonder whether she had done the right thing. But she wouldn't linger on that thought because she wanted everything to be right for Walter, whom she loved so much.

When Walter was nine, his mother, Ruby, and the two older children in the family moved back to Ipnatchiaq.

It was in 1928. Sikki was so happy to have her own family back in the same village. And the family could claim Walter again. There were no hard feelings, and all of the family were grateful to the Barrs for helping Sikki out with Walter.

At this time, Ruby and Clay Outwater, son of Neġroġruq, or Ne, Sikki's Storytelling friend, found each other and decided to get married. Sikki and Ne were very happy about the union, not only because they were friends, but also because each knew Ruby and Clay came from good families. They could be assured that their children would take good care of each other even after Sikki and Ne were no longer around.

Also at this time, Walter asked if he could go up north to visit his biological father, Murphy Johnson. Sikki knew that he had always wanted to do this, and so she gave her permission. Walter journeyed north to find out whether he could live with his father. But he discovered that too much time had passed and that the relationship wasn't what he expected. So he traveled home to Ipnatchiaq.

Sikki was very happy when she heard that Walter was coming home. She thought, if he can't live with his mother and new stepfather, maybe he can move back with me. It won't be so hard now that Walter is older and can do many things by himself.

When the day came Walter was expected to arrive by boat, Sikki walked to Magid's store and sat down on the bench in front, waiting for his boat to come in.

When Walter arrived, she asked him. "Will you be going back north?"

"No," he answered, "I'm home."

Sikki knew that her new son-in-law, Clay Outwater, was a kind man and truly wanted Walter to live with Ruby and him. He even told Walter that he could call him "Papa." Ruby told Sikki what was said. Sikki encouraged Walter to live with his mother and Clay if he wanted to. But he decided he would just spend time there. He felt that he wouldn't fit in now, since he had been raised by his grandmother ever since he could remember and then by the Barr family. So Walter lived with Sikki once again.

As the next two years went by, Sikki's son, Dick Mills, came back to Ipnatchiaq to help take care of Sikki. He wasn't with anyone at that time, but had been at Kaniq for a few years living with a widow. When that relationship failed, Dick returned to Ipnatchiaq, where he could help Sikki. She had become too old to chop her wood or to go upriver to get ice for her water. It was in 1932 and she was now fifty-three years old.

Sikki enjoyed having Walter living with her too. He still attended school, and Sikki knew that he would rather not go to school now that he was getting older. He and other young men of the village went out hunting whatever was in season, and so it was getting harder and harder for him to attend school.

One day in March of 1932, Sikki knew that she wouldn't be living much longer. She asked Walter to go out and bring her a ptarmigan so that she could taste it for the last time. Walter took his uncle's gun and went out hunting for a ptarmigan. When he got home, his uncle Dick plucked the ptarmigan and made some soup. That was Sikki's last meal.

Walter was proud that Sikki had relied on him for her final wish. Hunting ptarmigan was a wonderful memory they shared.

When Sikki died, Walter, whose name was now Walter Emuk Outwater, was about thirteen years old. Walter's uncle Dick moved on to Kotzebue, where he eventually settled down with a wife, Bessie, and child, Nettie.

Walter took a job at Charlie Okuda's restaurant and hotel. For two years, he worked there, bringing in ice for water and sweeping up the place. He lived there and went to school at the same time. Walter knew that his grandmother would be proud of him for working and going to school.

In the hotel, gold miners lived, who stayed in the village over the winter. The gold miners lived like there was no tomorrow. Walter thought about how, when living with Sikki, there was always a tomorrow. She was always looking forward to whatever they next would be hunting or fishing, or whatever greens or berries would be ready to harvest. The miners didn't have to go hunting or fishing to stay alive. They had money that they earned from gold mining, and they used that money to live and eat at Okuda's hotel. Walter thought about how that was so different from anything he and Sikki had experienced.

Walter grew to be a strong, independent adult, living well in two cultures. He married Ruth Savok in September 1938, when he was nineteen. He did many different kinds of work, from reindeer herding, gold mining, subsistence living, running the Ipnatchiaq general store, and operating heavy equipment to serving as assistant town manager, as well as serving in the Territorial Guard during World War II. He eventually became a Christian pastor, in 1961. Through the years, he lived in many places in Alaska: Koyuk, Wales, Nome, Kotzebue, and even Anchorage. But he was still tied to Ipnatchiaq (Deering), and returned there in 1992. At this writing, Walter was still alive.

Walter said, "Life was not easy." But he felt that he had gained much from living with his grandmother, Sikki, or Emma Sikkitkoq Mills, as he was growing up. He had been influenced by her and her friends, the Storytellers, and all the many relatives. He especially recalled how they reminded him to always help his elders. "I have received many blessings from doing that," Walter would say, with a gentle smile on his face.

REFERENCES

Ducker, James H. "Out of Harm's Way: Relocating Northwest Alaska Eskimos, 1907–1917." *American Indian Culture and Research Journal* 20(1):43–72, 1996.

National Library of Canada Holdings. The Search for Franklin and Franklin Relics 1847–1880. Session Papers, Houses of Parliament and Commons, London, England, 1847–. http://www.nlc-bcn.ca/ns-search/services/egovern.htm.

Ray, Dorothy Jean. *Ethnohistory in the Arctic: The Bering Strait Eskimo.* Fairbanks: University of Alaska Press, 1983.

Roberts, Arthur O. *Tomorrow is Growing Old: Stories of the Quakers in Alaska.* Newberg, Oregon: Barclay Press, 1978.

FAMILY PHOTOS

Emma Sikkitkoq (Sikki) Mills (1879–1932), photo date unknown. [PHOTO COURTESY OF EMMA HYDE AND RUTH OUTWATER]

▼ *Walter Emuk Outwater (1919–), right, with Fred Tipleman, left, and Frank Tipleman in front, ca. 1932.* [PHOTO COURTESY OF ESTHER TIPLEMAN]

◀ *Clay Outwater (ca. 1941), Ruby's husband, son of Ne, one of the Storytellers. Clay adopted Walter, who is the author's father.*
[PHOTO COURTESY OF LORETTA OUTWATER COX]

▼ *Sikki's daughters, Topsy Horn and Ruby Outwater, in Anchorage, Alaska, ca. 1972. Sikki raised Ruby's son, Emuk (Walter) for many years.* [PHOTO COURTESY OF LORETTA OUTWATER COX]

▲ Ruth and Walter Outwater's sixtieth anniversary, 1998, Anchorage, Alaska. The family gathering shows that Walter did indeed have many descendants, as foretold, including six daughters and many grandchildren. Walter and Ruth are seated in the center; Ruth is wearing white. The author, Loretta Outwater Cox, Walter's daughter, is seated to her mother's right. [PHOTO COURTESY OF CLARA VARIEUR]

About the Author

Loretta Outwater Cox is an Inupiaq Eskimo woman, born in Nome, Alaska, and raised in various villages around the Seward Peninsula. She holds a bachelor's degree in education and a master's degree in education administration. Loretta taught school in western Alaska for twenty-three years. She and her husband, Skip, live in Fairbanks. They have four children and seven grandchildren.